Anonymous

Ready References

A compilation of scripture texts arranged in subjective order, with numerous

annotations from eminent writers. Vol. 1

Anonymous

Ready References
A compilation of scripture texts arranged in subjective order, with numerous annotations from eminent writers. Vol. 1

ISBN/EAN: 9783337386160

Printed in Europe, USA, Canada, Australia, Japan

Cover: Foto ©Andreas Hilbeck / pixelio.de

More available books at **www.hansebooks.com**

READY REFERENCES,

A Compilation of Scripture Texts,

Arranged in Subjective Order, with Numerous
Annotations from Eminent
Writers.

— — — · —

DESIGNED ESPECIALLY FOR THE

Use of Missionaries and Scripture Students.

———————

SALT LAKE CITY, UTAH:
THE DESERET NEWS PUBLISHING CO., PRINTERS AND PUBLISHERS.
1892

PREFACE.

SOME months since a couple of humble Elders from Utah, laboring in the British Mission, began compiling a small volume each of Scripture texts for their own use, by clipping passages out of the Bible, arranging them in subjective order, and pasting them in memorandum books. Several considerations combined to induce them to do this. In the first place, their memories were not sufficiently retentive to enable them to quote literally, and give chapter and verse for all the passages required to support the various principles they were expected to preach upon in public, or converse with strangers about in private. Again, it was not always convenient to carry a Bible in the pocket, and if they did so, it was somewhat troublesome to turn to the various passages wanted in consecutive order. And finally they were expected to prove whatever they taught from the Bible, for, devoutly as these Elders believed in the more modern revelations of God to man, the people of England generally were not willing to concede their validity.

After compiling these small books, and finding them very handy in their labors, it occurred to them that if such a work were published, and especially if a few collateral notes from profane history, or from writers of accepted reliability, were added, it would be appreciated and found useful by others engaged as they were. With this in view, one of these Elders, who had some knowledge of the typographic art, applied himself during his odd moments, when not engaged with other duties, to the labor of setting the type for it in the *Millennial Star* office, and getting it stereotyped, four pages at a time. Others were ready to extend encouragement and some assistance in collecting the matter for the historical notes, and the result is the present volume, published by the Church of Jesus Christ of Latter-day Saints.

The Elders mentioned, in compiling and setting the type for the work, have performed their part as a labor of love, and with the hope that it may be issued at the lowest possible price (sufficient only to cover the cost of stereotyping, paper, press-work, and binding), they feel to dedicate it to the cause of God and to the especial use of the Elders who are laboring in the ministry.

42 ISLINGTON, LIVERPOOL,
  Nov. 15, 1884.

PREFACE TO THE THIRD EDITION.

THE first edition of this work met with a very ready sale in Great Britain, and gave much satisfaction to the missionaries and others who used it. Quite a number of copies were also imported to this Territory, which, however, so far from satisfying the public demand only seemed to increase it, so highly was the work appreciated by all into whose hands it chanced it fall. To meet the increasing demand without the trouble and expense of importing the books from abroad, THE DESERET NEWS COMPANY made application to the compilers for the privilege of publishing an edition here. This consent being given, an edition was issued which has already been sold, and we now present a third edition to the still unsatisfied public.

Some improvement has been made in the arrangement of the references, and a few passages have been added; otherwise this edition is similar to the former. That the work may prove acceptable to the public, and great good result from its more extensive publication, is the earnest desire of

THE PUBLISHERS.

SALT LAKE CITY,
    October 12, 1892.

CONTENTS.

ARTICLES OF FAITH, page 7.

THE GOSPEL, 9; Not of man, 10; Its antiquity, 12; Preached to the dead, 12; All to be judged by it, 13; Class of men called to preach, 13; Authority to preach, 15.

FAITH—What it is, 16; The principle of power, 17; In God, 18; In Jesus Christ, 19; In the Holy Ghost, 21; In the Gospel, 22; In the Priesthood, 23; Continuous revelation, 24; Necessity of faith, 25; Salvation promised through it, 26; Blessings promised, 27; Faith and works, 29.

REPENTANCE, 33; Two kinds, 34; Rewards promised, 36; Penalty of non-repentance, 36; All sinful, 38.

BAPTISM—A law of God, 39; Meaning of the word, and manner of ordinance—Notes from historians, 41; Compared to a burial and planting, 43; Object of it, 43; Proper subjects for, 44; Notes on infant baptism, 46: When sprinkling was inaugurated, 47.

THE HOLY GHOST promised, 48; Manifestations of the Spirit, 50; How conferred, 51; Notes from historians, 52.

LAYING ON HANDS for healing of sick, 53; To confer blessings, 55.

CHURCH ORGANIZATION—What it consists of, 56; Its officers, 56; Prophets and Apostles, 57; Evangelists and High Priests, 59; Seventies, 60; Bishops and Elders, 61; Priests, Teachers and Deacons, 62: Spiritual gifts, 62.

DIVINE AUTHORITY—Necessity of it, 64; Given to the Apostles 64; How conferred, 65.

APOSTASY FROM THE GOSPEL—Foretold, 67; Universal, 68; Internal causes, 69; External, 71; Present condition of the world, 72; Historical notes, 76.

RESTORATION OF THE GOSPEL, and the establishment of the Kingdom of God, 78; When to be restored, 79.

THE SCATTERING OF ISRAEL, 81; Reasons for the scattering, 82.

GATHERING OF ISRAEL, 83; To be gathered, 84: Where from, etc., 86; Promised inheritance, 90.

SECOND COMING OF CHRIST, 97; Signs to precede His coming, 98; How He will come, 100; Where He will come to, 101.

THE ATONEMENT, 102; Fore-ordained, 103; Original sin atoned for, 103; Application to personal sins, conditional, 105.

THE RESURRECTION, 106; Universal, 108; Order of it, 108; Different degrees of glory, 109; Judgment to follow the resurrection, 110.

PRE-EXISTENCE of Spirits, 115; Spirit of man immortal, 119.

PERSONALITY OF GOD, 120; Parts of the Deity mentioned, 122; Passions, 124.

SALVATION FOR THE DEAD, 125; Vicarious work upon earth in their behalf, 127; Historical notes, 128.

PATRIARCHAL MARRIAGE, 129; Plural marriage commanded by divine law and sanctioned by the Lord, 130; Polygamy predicted, 135; Notes on the subject, 136.

TITHING, 142; Persons to be benefitted by the tithes, 144; Prosperity resulting from paying tithes, 144.

PERSECUTION the heritage of the faithful, 146; Consolation in it, 147; Endured anciently, 148; Why the righteous are persecuted, 150.

DOOM OF APOSTATES, 151.

LATTER-DAY REVELATION AND MIRACLES, 152; Who are to receive it, 153; A New Covenant, 154; Church to be built on the Rock of Revelation, 156; Truth to spring out of the earth, 156; Sticks of Judah and Ephraim, 157; Seed of Israel to be known, 158; Latter-day signs and miracles, 160; Marvelous work to be done in the last days, 161.

THE PASSOVER OR SACRAMENT, 163; When and how to be kept, 163; Observed by Christ and His Apostles, 163; By His disciples, 164.

LOST SCRIPTURE—Scripture mentioned but not found in the Bible, 165.

ARTICLES OF FAITH

OF THE

CHURCH OF JESUS CHRIST OF LATTER-DAY SAINTS.

1 We believe in God, the Eternal Father, and in His Son Jesus Christ, and in the Holy Ghost.

PERSONALITY OF GOD.—Gen. i. 26, 27; v. 1; ix. 6; xviii.; xxxii 24-30; Ex. xxiv. 9, 11; xxxiii. 9-11, 20-23; Num. xii. 7, 8; John v. 19, 20; Acts vii. 55, 56; Phil. ii. 5-8; Heb i. 3.

PERSONALITY OF CHRIST.—Matt. iii. 17; John v. 26, 27; xv.; xvi. xvii.; 1 Tim. ii. 5; 1 John v. 7.

HOLY GHOST.—Isaiah xi. 1-3; lxi. 1; Matt. iii. 16; Mark i. 10; Luke iii. 22; John i. 32, 33; xvi. 13, 14; Acts i. 5; ii. 4; viii. 17-19; xix. 2-6.

2. We believe that men will be punished for their own sins, and not for Adam's transgression.

MAN PUNISHED FOR ACTUAL SINS.—Jer. xvii. 10; Matt. xii. 36, 37; xvi. 27; 2 Cor. v. 10. ; Rev. xx. 12-15,

3. We believe that through the atonement of Christ, all mankind may be saved, by obedience to the laws and ordinances of the Gospel.

ATONEMENT OF CHRIST.—Isa. liii.; Acts iv. 12; Rom. v. 12-19 1 John i. 7-10.

4. We believe that these ordinances are: first, Faith in the Lord Jesus Christ; second, Repentance; third, Baptism by immersion for the remission of sins; fourth, Laying on of hands for the Gift of the Holy Ghost.

FAITH, REPENTANCE, BAPTISM AND LAYING ON HANDS.—Heb. xi; Rom. i, 16, 17; x. 14, 15; Jas. ii. 14-26; Mark xvi. 15, 16; Acts ii. 38, 39; 2 Cor. vii. 9, 10; Isa. lv. 6, 7; Eph. iv. 25-32; Luke xiii. 3; Matt. iv. 17; Acts viii. 14-17; xix. 1-6; John iii. 5; Heb. vi. 1, 2.

5. We believe that a man must be called of God, by "prophecy and by the laying on of hands," by those who are in authority, to preach the Gospel and administer in the ordinances thereof.

CALLED OF GOD.—Mark iii. 14; John xv. 16; xvii. 18; Acts xiii. 1-4; xiv. 23; Rom. x. 14, 15; Gal. i. 8-16; 1 Tim. ii. 7; Heb. iii. 1; v. 4-10; 1 Peter ii. 5-9; Rev. v. 9, 10.

6. We believe in the same organization that existed in the primitive church, viz: apostles, prophets, pastors, teachers, evangelists, etc.

ORGANIZATION.—1 Cor. xii.; Eph. ii. 19-22; iv.

7. We believe in the gift of tongues, prophecy, revelation, visions, healing, interpretation of tongues, etc.

SPIRITUAL GIFTS.—Mark xvi. 15-20; John xiv. 12; Acts ii. 17; 1 Cor. xii.; 1 Thess. v. 19, 20; James v. 14, 15.

8. We believe the Bible to be the Word of God, as far as it is translated correctly; we also believe the Book of Mormon to be the word of God.

BOOK OF MORMON.—Isaiah xxix. 4, 9-24; Ezekiel xxxvii. 15-28; Hosea viii. 12; John x. 16.

9. We believe all that God has revealed, all that He does now reveal, and we believe that He will yet reveal many great and important things pertaining to the kingdom of God.

LATTER-DAY REVELATIONS.—Ezekiel xx. 35, 36; Joel ii. 28, 29; Amos iii. 7; Mic. ii. 6, 7; Mal. iii. 1-4; iv.; Acts ii. 17, 18; Jas. i. 5, 6; Rev. xiv. 6.

10. We believe in the literal gathering of Israel and the restoration of the Ten Tribes. That Zion will be built upon this (the American) continent. That Christ will reign personally upon the earth, and that the earth will be renewed and receive its paradisaic glory.

GATHERING.—Neh. i. 8, 9; Ps. l. 5; cvii. 1-7; Isa. ii. 2, 3; v. 26, 27; xi. 11-16; xliii. 5-9; xlix, 12; lx. 4, 5; Jer. iii. 14, 15; xvi. 14-16; xxiii. 3-8; xxx. 1-8; xxxi. 8-12; xxxii. 37-39; l. 4, 5; Ezek. xx. 33-38; xxxix. 28; Zech. xiv.; Matt. xxiv. 31; John xi, 52; Eph. i. 10; Rev. xviii. 4.

11. We claim the privilege of worshiping Almighty God according to the dictates of our conscience, and allow all men the same privilege, let them worship how, where or what they may.

12. We believe in being subject to kings, presidents, rulers and magistrates, in obeying, honoring and sustaining the law.

13. We believe in being honest, true, chaste, benevolent, virtuous, and in doing good to all men; indeed, we may say that we follow the admonition of Paul, "We believe all things, we hope all things," we have endured many things, and hope to be able to endure all things. If there is anything virtuous, lovely or of good report, or praiseworthy, we seek after these things.—JOSEPH SMITH.

READY REFERENCES.

THE GOSPEL.

16. For I am not ashamed of the Gospel of *What it is:* Christ: for it is the power of God unto salvation to every one that believeth; to the Jew first, and also to the Greek.

17. For therein is the righteousness of God revealed from faith to faith: as it is written, The just shall live by faith.—*Rom.* 1.

1. The beginning of the Gospel of Jesus Christ, the Son of God;

4. John did baptize in the wilderness, and preach the baptism of repentance for the remission of sins.

5. And there went out unto him all the land of Judæa, and they of Jerusalem, and were all baptized of him in the river of Jordan, confessing their sins.

7. And preached, saying, There cometh one mightier than I after me, the latchet of whose shoes I am not worthy to stoop down and unloose.

8. I indeed have baptized you with water: but he shall baptize you with the Holy Ghost. —*Mark* 1.

14. And this Gospel of the kingdom shall *To be* be preached in all the world for a witness unto *Preached:* all nations; and then shall the end come.— *Matt.* 24.

2

And Published: 10. And the Gospel must first be published among all nations.—*Mark* 13.

Preached by Jesus: 14. Now after that John was put in prison, Jesus came into Galilee, preaching the Gospel of the kingdom of God,

15. And saying, The time is fulfilled, and the kingdom of God is at hand: repent ye, and believe the Gospel.—*Mark* 1.

Apostles Commanded: 15. And he said unto them, Go ye into all the world, and preach the Gospel to every creature.—*Mark* 16.

Only one Gospel: 8. But though we, or an angel from heaven, preach any other Gospel unto you than that which we have preached unto you, let him be accursed.—*Gal.* 1.

4. There is one body, and one spirit, even as ye are called in one hope of your calling;

5. One Lord, one faith, one baptism,

6. One God, one Father of all, who is above all, and through all, and in you all.—*Eph.* 4.

Not of man: 11. But I certify you, brethren, that the Gospel which was preached of me is not after man.

12. For I neither received it of man, neither was I taught it, but by the revelation of Jesus Christ.—*Gal.* 1.

Is not Discerned by our Natural Senses: 14. But the natural man receiveth not the things of the Spirit of God: for they are foolishness unto him: neither can he know them, because they are spiritually discerned.

11. For what man knoweth the things of a man, save the spirit of man which is in him? even so the things of God knoweth no man, but the Spirit of God.—1 *Cor.* 2.

Not Acceptable to the World: 18. For the preaching of the cross is to them that perish foolishness; but unto us which are saved it is the power of God.—1 *Cor.* 1.

21. For after that in the wisdom of God the world by wisdom knew not God, it pleased God by the foolishness of preaching to save them that believe.—1 *Cor.* 1.

Not Acceptable to the World.

3. But if our Gospel be hid, it is hid to them that are lost:

4. In whom the god of this world hath blinded the minds of them which believe not, lest the light of the glorious Gospel of Christ, who is the image of God, should shine unto them.—2 *Cor.* 4.

22. But we desire to hear of thee what thou thinkest: for as concerning this sect, we know that every where it is spoken against.—*Acts.* 28.

16. Jesus answered them, and said, My doctrine is not mine, but his that sent me.

17. If any man will do his will, he shall know of the doctrine, whether it be of God, or whether I speak of myself.—*John* 7.

How a knowledge is to be obtained:

3. How that by revelation he made known unto me the mystery;

5. Which in other ages was not made known unto the sons of men, as it is now revealed unto his holy apostles and prophets by the Spirit.— *Eph.* 3.

By Revelation:

12. For I neither received it of man, neither was I taught it, but by the revelation of Jesus Christ.—*Gal.* 1.

16. The Spirit itself beareth witness with our spirit, that we are the children of God.— *Rom.* 8.

9. But as it is written, Eye hath not seen, nor ear heard, neither have entered into the heart of man, the things which God hath prepared for them that love him.—1 *Cor.* 2.

By Revelation: 10. But God hath revealed them unto us by his Spirit: for the Spirit searcheth all things, yea, the deep things of God.—1 *Cor.* 2.

Preached to Abraham: 8. And the scripture, foreseeing that God would justify the heathen through faith, preached before the Gospel unto Abraham, saying, In thee shall all nations be blessed.—*Gal.* 3.

To the Israelites under Moses: 2. For unto us was the Gospel preached, as well as unto them: but the word preached did not profit them, not being mixed with faith in them that heard it.—*Heb.* 4.

Preached to the dead: 25. Verily, verily, I say unto you, The hour is coming, and now is, when the dead shall hear the voice of the Son of God: and they that hear shall live.—*John* 5.

18. For Christ also hath once suffered for sins, the just for the unjust, that he might bring us to God, being put to death in the flesh, but quickened by the Spirit:

19. By which also he went and preached unto the spirits in prison;

20. Which sometime were disobedient, when once the longsuffering of God waited in the days of Noah, while the ark was a preparing, wherein few, that is, eight souls were saved by water.—1 *Pet.* 3.

6. For, for this cause was the Gospel preached also to them that are dead, that they might be judged according to men in the flesh, but live according to God in the Spirit.—1 *Pet.* 4.

Universal: 10. And the Gospel must first be published among all nations.—*Mark* 13.

14. And this Gospel of the kingdom shall be preached in all the world for a witness unto all nations; and then shall the end come.—*Matt.* 24.

15. And he said unto them, go ye into all the world, and preach the Gospel to every creature.—*Mark* 16.

16. In the day when God shall judge the secrets of men by Jesus Christ according to my Gospel.—*Rom.* 2.

To be Judged by it:

48. He that rejecteth me, and receiveth not my words, hath one that judgeth him: the word that I have spoken, the same shall judge him in the last day.

49. For I have not spoken of myself; but of the Father which sent me, he gave me a commandment, what I would say, and what I should speak.

50. And I know that his commandment is life everlasting: whatsoever I speak therefore, even as the father said unto me, so I speak.—*John* 12.

17. For the time is come that judgment must begin at the house of God: and if it first begin at us, what shall the end be of them that obey not the Gospel of God?

18. And if the righteous scarcely be saved, where shall the ungodly and sinner appear? —1 *Pet.* 4.

7. And to you who are troubled rest with us, when the Lord Jesus shall be revealed from heaven with his mighty angels,

8. In flaming fire taking vengeance on them that know not God, and that obey not the Gospel of our Lord Jesus Christ:

9. Who shall be punished with everlasting destruction from the presence of the Lord, and from the glory of his power.—2 *Thes.* 1.

18. And Jesus, walking by the sea of Galilee, saw two brethren, Simon called Peter, and Andrew his brother, casting a net into the sea: for they were fishers.—*Matt.* 4.

Class of men Called to Preach:

Class of men
Called to
Preach:
19. And he saith unto them, Follow me, and I will make you fishers of men.—*Matt.* 4.

9. And as Jesus passed forth from thence, he saw a man, named Matthew, sitting at the receipt of custom: and he saith unto him, Follow me. And he arose and followed him.—*Matt.* 9.

26. For ye see your calling, brethren, how that not many wise men after the flesh, not many mighty, not many noble, are called:

27. But God hath chosen the foolish things of the world to confound the wise; and God hath chosen the weak things of the world to confound the things which are mighty;

28. And base things of the world, and things which are despised, hath God chosen, yea, and things which are not, to bring to naught things that are:

The reason
why:
29. That no flesh should glory in his presence.—1 *Cor.* 1.

Obligation
to Preach:
16. For though I preach the Gospel, I have nothing to glory of: for necessity is laid upon me; yea, woe is ui to me, if I preach not the Gospel!—1 *Cor.* 9.

17. Son of man, I have made thee a watchman unto the house of Israel: therefore hear the word at my mouth, and give them warning from me.

18. When I say unto the wicked, thou shalt surely die; and thou givest him not warning, nor speakest to warn the wicked from his wicked way, to save his life; the same wicked man shall die in his iniquity; but his blood will I require at thine hand.

19. Yet if thou warn the wicked, and he turn not from his wickedness, nor from his wicked way, he shall die in his iniquity; but thou hast delivered thy soul.—*Ezek.* 3.

3. Therefore, whatsoever ye have spoken in darkness, shall be heard in the light; and that which ye have spoken in the ear in closets shall be proclaimed upon the housetops.—*Luke* 12.

Men Answerable for their Teachings:

36. But I say unto you, that every idle word that men shall speak, they shall give account thereof in the day of judgment.—*Matt.* 12.

14. How then shall they call on him in whom they have not believed? and how shall they believe in him of whom they have not heard? and how shall they hear without a preacher?

Authority to Preach:

15. And how shall they preach, except they be sent?—*Rom.* 10.

16. Ye have not chosen me, but I have chosen you, and ordained you, that ye should go and bring forth fruit, and that your fruit should remain: that whatsoever ye shall ask of the Father in my name, he may give it you.—*John* 15.

4. And no man taketh this honor unto himself, but he that is called of God, as was Aaron. —*Heb.* 5.

Or act in the name of the Lord:

14. And the anger of the Lord was kindled against Moses, and he said, Is not Aaron the Levite thy brother? I know that he can speak well. And also, behold, he cometh forth to meet thee: and when he seeth thee, he will be glad in his heart.

How Aaron was called:

15. And thou shalt speak unto him, and put words into his mouth: and I will be with thy mouth, and with his mouth, and will teach you what ye shall do.

16. And he shall be thy spokesman unto the people: and he shall be, even he shall be to thee instead of a mouth, and thou shalt be to him instead of God.—*Ex.* 4.

FAITH.

THE FIRST PRINCIPLE OF THE GOSPEL.

Paul's Testimony: 16. For I am not ashamed of the Gospel of Christ: for it is the power of God unto salvation to every one that believeth; to the Jew first, and also to the Greek.

17. For therein is the righteousness of God revealed from faith to faith: as it is written, The just shall live by faith.—*Rom.* 1.

What Faith is: 1. Now faith is the substance of things hoped for, the evidence of things not seen.—*Heb.* 11.

Foundation of the doctrine of Christ: 1. Therefore leaving the principles of the doctrine of Christ, let us go on unto perfection; not laying again the foundation of repentance from dead works, and of faith toward God.—*Heb.* 6.

Fruit of the Spirit: 22. But the fruit of the Spirit is love, joy, peace, longsuffering, gentleness, goodness, faith. —*Gal.* 5.

Moving Cause of all action: 7. By faith Noah, being warned of God of things not seen as yet, moved with fear, prepared an ark to the saving of his house; by the which he condemned the world, and became heir of the righteousness which is by faith.

8. By faith Abraham, when he was called to go out into a place which he should after receive for an inheritance, obeyed; and he went out, not knowing whither he went.

9. By faith he sojourned in the land of promise, as in a strange country, dwelling in tabernacles with Isaac and Jacob, the heirs with him of the same promise:

10. For he looked for a city which hath foundations, whose builder and maker is God. —*Heb.* 11.

11. Through faith also Sara herself received strength to conceive seed, and was delivered of a child when she was past age, because she judged him faithful who had promised.

Moving Cause of all action:

17. By faith Abraham, when he was tried, offered up Isaac: and he that had received the promises offered up his only begotten son,

18. Of whom it was said, That in Isaac shall thy seed be called:

19. Accounting that God was able to raise him up, even from the dead; from whence also he received him in a figure.

24. By faith Moses, when he was come to years, refused to be called the son of Pharaoh's daughter;

25. Choosing rather to suffer affliction with the people of God, then to enjoy the pleasures of sin for a season;

26. Esteeming the reproach of Christ greater riches than the treasures in Egypt: for he had respect unto the recompense of the reward.

27. By faith he forsook Egypt, not fearing the wrath of the king: for he endured, as seeing him who is invisible.—*Heb.* 11.

18. Yea, a man may say, Thou hast faith, and I have works: show me thy faith without thy works, and I will show thee my faith by my works.—*Jas.* 2.

The Principle of Power:

3. Through faith we understand that the worlds were framed by the word of God, so that things which are seen were not made of things which do appear.

29. By faith they passed through the Red sea as by dry land: which the Egyptians assaying to do were drowned.

30. By faith the walls of Jericho fell down, after they were compassed about seven days.—*Heb.* 11.

The Principle of Power:

32. And what shall I more say? for the time would fail me to tell of Gedeon, and of Barak, and of Samson, and of Jephthae; of David also, and Samuel, and of the prophets:

33. Who through faith subdued kingdoms, wrought righteousness, obtained promises, stopped the mouths of lions,

34. Quenched the violence of fire, escaped the edge of the sword, out of weakness were made strong, waxed valiant in fight, turned to flight the armies of the aliens.—*Heb.* 11.

Nothing impossible with faith:

19. Then came the disciples to Jesus apart, and said, Why could not we cast him out?

20. And Jesus said unto them, Because of your unbelief: for verily I say unto you, If ye have faith as a grain of mustard seed, ye shall say unto this mountain, Remove hence to yonder place; and it shall remove; and nothing shall be impossible unto you.—*Matt.* 17.

23. Jesus said unto him, If thou canst believe, all things are possible to him that believeth.—*Mark* 9.

16. Above all, taking the shield of faith, wherewith ye shall be able to quench all the fiery darts of the wicked.—*Eph.* 6.

4. For whatsoever is born of God overcometh the world: and this is the victory that overcometh the world, even our faith.

5. Who is he that overcometh the world, but he that believeth that Jesus is the Son of God? —1 *John* 5.

Faith in God:

9. But we had the sentence of death in ourselves, that we should not trust in ourselves, but in God which raiseth the dead:

10. Who delivered us from so great a death, and doth deliver: in whom we trust that he will yet deliver us.—2 *Cor.* 1.

6. But without faith it is impossible to please *Faith in God:*
him: for he that cometh to God must believe
that he is, and that he is a rewarder of them
that diligently seek him.—*Heb.* 11.

24. Verily, verily, I say unto you, He that
heareth my word, and believeth on him that
sent me, hath everlasting life, and shall not
come into condemnation; but is passed from
death unto life.—*John* 5.

3. And this is life eternal, that they might
know thee the only true God, and Jesus Christ,
whom thou hast sent.—*John* 17.

22. All things are delivered to me of my
Father: and no man knoweth who the Son is,
but the Father; and who the Father is, but the
Son, and he to whom the Son will reveal him.
—*Luke* 10.

10. For therefore we both labor and suffer
reproach, because we trust in the living God,
who is the Savior of all men, specially of those
that believe.— 1 *Tim.* 4.

18. Forasmuch as ye know that ye were not
redeemed with corruptible things, as silver and
gold, from your vain conversation received by
tradition from your fathers;
19. But with the precious blood of Christ, as
of a lamb without blemish and without spot:
20. Who verily was foreordained before the
foundation of the world, but was manifest in
these last times for you,
21. Who by him do believe in God, that raised
him up from the dead, and gave him glory; that
your faith and hope might be in God.—1 *Pet.* 1.

36. He that believeth on the Son hath ever- *Faith in Jesus Christ:*
lasting life: and he that believeth not the Son
shall not see life; but the wrath of God abideth
on him.—*John* 3.

1. Let not your heart be troubled: ye believe in God, believe also in me.

11. Believe me that I am in the Father, and the Father in me: or else believe me for the very works' sake.

12. Verily, verily, I say unto you, He that believeth on me, the works that I do shall he do also; and greater works than these shall he do; because I go unto my Father.—*John* 14.

30. And many other signs truly did Jesus in the presence of his disciples, which are not written in this book:

31. But these are written, that ye might believe that Jesus is the Christ, the Son of God; and that believing ye might have life through his name.—*John* 20.

12. Neither is there salvation in any other: for there is none other name under heaven given among men, whereby we must be saved. —*Acts* 4.

23. And this is his commandment, That we should believe on the name of his Son Jesus Christ, and love one another, as he gave us commandment.

24. And he that keepeth his commandments dwelleth in him, and he in him. And hereby we know that he abideth in us, by the Spirit which he hath given us.—1 *John* 3.

10. He that believeth on the Son of God hath the witness in himself: He that believeth not God hath made him a liar; because he believeth not the record that God gave of his Son.

11. And this is the record, that God hath given to us eternal life, and this life is in his Son.

12. He that hath the Son hath life; and he that hath not the Son of God hath not life.—1 *John* 5.

13. These things I have written unto you *Faith in* that believe on the name of the Son of God; *Jesus Christ:* that ye may know that ye have eternal life, and that ye may believe on the name of the Son of God.—1 *John* 5.

11. And when they bring you into the syn- *Faith in* agogues, and unto magistrates, and powers, *Holy Ghost:* take ye no thought how or what thing ye shall answer, or what ye shall say:

12. For the Holy Ghost shall teach you in the same hour what ye ought to say.—*Luke* 12.

13. Howbeit when he, the Spirit of truth, is come, he will guide you into all truth: for he shall not speak of himself; but whatsoever he shall hear, that shall he speak: and he will show you things to come.

14. He shall glorify me: for he shall receive of mine, and shall show it unto you.—*John* 16.

8. But ye shall receive power, after that the Holy Ghost is come upon you: and ye shall be witnesses unto me both in Jerusalem, and in all Judæa, and in Samaria, and unto the uttermost part of the earth.—*Acts* 1.

32. And we are his witnesses of these things; and so is also the Holy Ghost, whom God hath given to them that obey him.—*Acts* 5.

38. How God anointed Jesus of Nazareth with the Holy Ghost and with power: who went about doing good, and healing all that were oppressed of the devil; for God was with him.—*Acts.* 10.

15. And as I began to speak, the Holy Ghost fell on them, as on us at the beginning.

16. Then remembered I the word of the Lord, how that he said, John indeed baptized with water; but ye shall be baptized with the Holy Ghost.—*Acts* 11.

Faith in Holy Ghost: 17. Forasmuch then as God gave them the like gift as he did unto us, who believed on the Lord Jesus Christ; what was I, what I could withstand God?—*Acts* 11.

26. But the comforter, which is the Holy Ghost, whom the father will send in my name, he shall teach you all things, and bring all things to your remembrance, whatsoever I have said unto you.—*John* 14.

7 For there are three that bear record in heaven, the Father, the Word, and the Holy Ghost: and these three are one.—1 *John* 5.

Faith in the Gospel: 13. For this cause also thank we God without ceasing, because, when ye received the word of God which ye heard of us, ye received it not as the word of men, but as it is in truth, the word of God, which effectually worketh also in you that believe.—1 *Thes.* 2.

2. For unto us was the Gospel preached, as well as unto them: but the word preached did not profit them, not being mixed with faith in them that heard it.—*Heb.* 4.

19. We have also a more sure word of prophecy; whereunto ye do well that ye take heed, as unto a light that shineth in a dark place, until the day dawn, and the day star arise in your hearts:

20. Knowing this first, that no prophecy of the scripture is of any private interpretation.

21. For the prophecy came not in old time by the will of man: but holy men of God spake as they were moved by the Holy Ghost.—2 *Pet.* 1.

45. Do not think that I will accuse you to the Father: there is one that accuseth you, even Moses, in whom ye trust.—*John* 5.

46. For had ye believed Moses, ye would have *Faith in the Gospel:* believed me: for he wrote of me.

47. But if ye believe not his writings, how shall ye believe my words?—*John* 5.

20. And they rose early in the morning, and *Faith in the Priesthood:* went forth into the wilderness of Tekoa: and as they went forth, Jehoshaphat stood and said, Hear me, O Judah, and ye inhabitants of Jerusalem; Believe in the Lord your God, so shall ye be established; believe his prophets, so shall ye prosper.—2 *Chr.* 20.

14. And whosoever shall not receive you, nor hear your words, when ye depart out of that house or city, shake off the dust of your feet.

15. Verily I say unto you, It shall be more tolerable for the land of Sodom and Gomorrah in the day of judgment, than for that city.

40. He that receiveth you receiveth me, and he that receiveth me receiveth him that sent me.

41. He that receiveth a prophet in the name of a prophet shall receive a prophet's reward; and he that receiveth a righteous man in the name of a righteous man shall receive a righteous man's reward.—*Matt.* 10.

16. He that heareth you heareth me; and he that despiseth you despiseth me; and he that despiseth me despiseth him that sent me.— *Luke* 10.

7. Remember them which have the rule over you, who have spoken unto you the word of God: whose faith follow, considering the end of their conversation.—*Heb.* 13.

18. Verily I say unto you, Whatsoever ye shall bind on earth shall be bound in heaven: and whatsoever ye shall loose on earth shall be loosed in heaven.—*Matt.* 18.

Faith in the Priesthood: 7. Surely the Lord God will do nothing, but he revealeth his secret unto his servants the prophets.

8. The lion hath roared, who will not fear? the Lord God hath spoken, who can but prophesy?—*Amos* 3.

Faith in Continuous Revelation: 29. And Moses said unto him, Enviest thou for my sake? would God that all the Lord's people were prophets, and that the Lord would put his Spirit upon them!—*Num.* 11.

17. And Jesus answered and said unto him, Blessed art thou, Simon Bar-jona: for flesh and blood hath not revealed it unto thee but my Father which is in heaven.

18. And I say also unto thee, that thou art Peter, and upon this rock I will build my church; and the gates of hell shall not prevail against it.—*Matt.* 16.

22. All things are delivered to me of my Father: and no man knoweth who the Son is, but the Father; and who the Father is, but the Son, and he to whom the Son will reveal him. —*Luke* 10.

8. Charity never faileth: but whether there be prophecies, they shall fail; whether there be tongues, they shall cease; whether there be knowledge, it shall vanish away.

9. For we know in part, and we prophesy in part.

10. But when that which is perfect is come, then that which is in part shall be done away.—1 *Cor.* 13.

17. That the God of our Lord Jesus Christ, the Father of glory, may give unto you the spirit of wisdom and revelation in the knowledge of him.—*Eph.* 1.

18. Where there is no vision the people perish: but he that keepeth the law, happy is he. —*Prov.* 29.

Faith in Continuous Revelation:

5. If any of you lack wisdom, let him ask of God, that giveth to all men liberally and upbraideth not; and it shall be given him.

6. But let him ask in faith, nothing wavering. For he that wavereth is like a wave of the sea driven with the wind and tossed.— *Jas.* 1.

15. And he said unto them, go ye into all the world, and preach the Gospel to every creature.

Necessity of it:

16. He that believeth and is baptized shall be saved; but he that believeth not shall be damned.—*Mark* 16.

16. For God so loved the world, that he gave his only begotten Son, that whosoever believeth in him should not perish, but have everlasting life.

17. For God sent not his Son into the world to condemn the world; but that the world through him might be saved.

18. He that believeth on him is not condemned: but he that believeth not is condemned already, because he hath not believed in the name of the only begotten Son of God. —*John* 3.

24. I said therefore unto you, that ye shall die in your sins: for if ye believe not that I am he, ye shall die in your sins.—*John* 8.

17. But with whom was he grieved forty years? Was it not with them that had sinned, whose carcasses fell in the wilderness?

18. And to whom sware he that they should not enter into his rest, but to them that believed not?—*Heb.* 3.

Necessity of it: 19. So we see that they could not enter in because of unbelief.—*Heb.* 3.

6. But without faith it is impossible to please him: for he that cometh to God must believe that he is, and that he is a rewarder of them that diligently seek him.—*Heb.* 11.

14 How then shall they call on him in whom they have not believed? and how shall they believe in him of whom they have not heard? and how shall they hear without a preacher?—*Rom.* 10.

How obtained: 8. And Crispus, the chief ruler of the synagogue, believed on the Lord with all his house; and many of the Corinthians hearing believed, and were baptized.—*Acts* 18.

17. So then faith cometh by hearing, and hearing by the word of God.—*Rom.* 10.

8. For to one is given by the Spirit the word of wisdom; to another the word of knowledge by the same Spirit;

9. To another faith by the same Spirit; to another the gifts of healing by the same Spirit. —1 *Cor.* 12.

19. Then came the disciples to Jesus apart, and said, Why could not we cast him out?

20. And Jesus said unto them, Because of your unbelief: for verily I say unto you, If ye have faith as a grain of mustard seed, ye shall say unto this mountain, Remove hence to yonder place; and it shall remove; and nothing shall be impossible unto you.

21. Howbeit, this kind goeth not out, but by prayer and fasting.—*Matt.* 17.

Salvation promised: 16. He that believeth and is baptized shall be saved; but he that believeth not shall be damned.—*Mark* 16.

16. For God so loved the world, that he *Salvation Promised:* gave his only b.gotten Son, that whosoever believeth on him should not perish, but have everlasting life.—*John* 3.

16. For I am not ashamed of the Gospel of Christ: for it is the power of God unto salvation to every one that believeth; to the Jew first, and also to the Greek.—*Rom.* 1.

8. But what saith it? The word is nigh thee, even in thy mouth,and in thy heart: that is, the word of faith, which we preach,

9. That if thou shalt confess with thy mouth the Lord Jesus, and shalt believe in thine heart that God hath raised him from the dead, thou shalt be saved.—*Rom.* 10.

21. For after that in the wisdom of God the world by wisdom knew not God, it pleased God by the foolishness of preaching to save them that believe.—1 *Cor.* 1.

9. Receiving the end of your faith, even the salvation of your souls.—1 *Peter* 1.

10. For therefore we both labor and suffer reproach, because we trust in the living God, who is the Savior of all men, especially of those that believe.—1 *Tim.* 4.

8. For by grace are ye saved, through faith; and that not of yourselves: *it is* the gift of God.—*Eph.* 2.

38. Now the just shall live by faith: but if any man draw back, my soul shall have no pleasure in him.

39. But we are not of them who draw back unto perdition; but of them that believe to the saving of the soul.—*Heb.* 10.

24. Therefore I say unto you, What things *Blessings Promised:* soever ye desire, when ye pray, believe that ye receive them,and ye shall have them.—*Mark* 11.

Blessings　　 17. And these signs shall follow them that
Promised: believe; in my name they shall cast out devils;
they shall speak with new tongues;

18. They shall take up serpents; and if they
drink any deadly thing it shall not hurt them;
they shall lay hands on the sick, and they shall
recover.—*Mark* 16.

12. But as many as received him, to them
gave he power to become the sons of God, even
to them that believe on his name.—*John* 1.

43. To him give all the prophets witness,
that through his name whosoever believeth in
him shall receive remission of sins.—*Acts* 10.

1. Therefore being justified by faith, we
have peace with God through our Lord Jesus
Christ:
2. By whom also we have access by faith
into this grace wherein we stand, and rejoice in
hope of the glory of God.—*Rom.* 5.

7. Know ye therefore that they which are of
faith, the same are the children of Abraham.
8. And the scripture, foreseeing that God
would justify the heathen through faith,
preached before the Gospel unto Abraham,
saying, In thee shall all nations be blessed.
9. So then they which be of faith are blessed
with faithful Abraham.
14. That the blessing of Abraham might
come on the Gentiles through Jesus Christ;
that we might receive the promise of the Spirit
through faith.—*Gal.* 3.

5. Hearken, my beloved brethren, Hath not
God chosen the poor of this world rich in faith,
and heirs of the kingdom which he hath promised to them that love him.—*Jas.* 2.

FAITH AND WORKS,

OR OBEDIENCE TO THE GOSPEL.

21. Not every one that saith unto me, Lord, Lord, shall enter into the kingdom of heaven; but he that doeth the will of my Father which is in heaven.—*Matt.* 7.

Words of the Savior:

16. Jesus answered them, and said, my doctrine is not mine, but his that sent me.
17. If any man will do his will, he shall know of the doctrine, whether it be of God, or whether I speak of myself.—*John* 7.

31. Then said Jesus to those Jews which believed on him, If ye continue in my word, then are ye my disciples indeed;
32. And ye shall know the truth, and the truth shall make you free.—*John* 8.

12. Verily, verily, I say unto you, He that believeth on me, the works that I do shall he do also; and greater works than these shall he do; because I go unto my Father.
15. If ye love me, keep my commandments.
21. He that hath my commandments, and keepeth them, he it is that loveth me: and he that loveth me shall be loved of my Father, and I will love him, and will manifest myself to him.—*John* 14.

7. And to you who are troubled rest with us, when the Lord Jesus shall be revealed from heaven with his mighty angels,
8. In flaming fire taking vengeance on them that know not God, and that obey not the gospel of our Lord Jesus Christ.—2 *Thes.* 1.

Paul's
Words: 8. This is a faithful saying, and these things I will that thou affirm constantly, that they which have believed in God might be careful to maintain good works. These things are good and profitable unto men.—*Titus* 3.

8. Though he were a Son, yet learned he obedience by the things which he suffered;

9. And being made perfect, he became the author of eternal salvation unto all them that obey him.—*Heb.* 5.

6. Who will render to every man according to his deeds:

7. To them who by patient continuance in well doing seek for glory and honor and immortality, eternal life:

8. But unto them that are contentious, and do not obey the truth, but obey unrighteousness, indignation and wrath.—*Rom.* 2.

16. Know ye not, that to whom ye yield yourselves servants to obey, his servants ye are to whom ye obey; whether of sin unto death, or of obedience unto righteousness?

17. But God be thanked, that ye were the servants of sin, but ye have obeyed from the heart that form of doctrine which was delivered you.

18. Being then made free from sin, ye became the servants of righteousness.—*Rom.* 6.

Words of
James: 22. But be ye doers of the word and not hearers only, deceiving your own selves.

23. For if any be a hearer of the word, and not a doer, he is like unto a man beholding his natural face in a glass:

24. For he beholdeth himself, and goeth his way, and straightway forgetteth what manner of man he was.—*Jas.* 1.

25. But whoso looketh into the perfect law of *Words of James*
liberty, and continueth therein, he being not
a forgetful hearer, but a doer of the work,
this man shall be blessed in his deed.—*Jas.* 1.

14. What doth it profit, my brethren, though
a man say he hath faith, and have not works?
can faith save him?

15. If a brother or sister be naked, and
destitute of daily food,

16. And one of you say unto them, Depart
in peace, be ye warmed and filled; notwithstanding ye give them not those things which
are needful to the body; what doth it profit?

17. Even so faith, if it hath not works, is
dead, being alone.

18. Yea, a man may say, Thou hast faith,
and I have works: shew me thy faith without
thy works, and I will shew thee my faith by
my works.

19. Thou believest that there is one God;
thou doest well: the devils also believe, and
tremble.

20. But wilt thou know, O vain man, that
faith without works is dead?

21. Was not Abraham our father justified by
works when he had offered Isaac his son upon
the altar?

22. Seest thou how faith wrought with his
works, and by works was faith made perfect?

23. And the scripture was fulfilled which
saith, Abraham believed God, and it was im-
puted unto him for righteousness: and he was
called the Friend of God.

24. Ye see then how that by works a man is
justified, and not by faith only.

26. For as the body without the spirit is
dead, so faith without works is dead also.—
Jas. 2.

Words of James: 13. Who *is* a wise man and endued with knowledge among you? let him shew out of a good conversation his works with meekness of wisdom.—*Jas.* 3.

17. Therefore to him that knoweth to do good, and doeth it not, to him it is sin.—*Jas.* 4.

John's Words: 5. This then is the message which we have heard of him, and declare unto you, that God is light, and in him is no darkness at all.

6. If we say that we have fellowship with him, and walk in darkness, we lie, and do not the truth:

7. But if we walk in the light, as he is in the light, we have fellowship one with another, and the blood of Jesus Christ his son cleanseth us from all sin.—1 *John* 1.

3. And hereby we do know that we know him, if we keep his commandments.

4. He that saith, I know him, and keepeth not his commandments, is a liar, and the truth is not in him.

5. But whoso keepeth his word, in him verily is the love of God perfected: hereby know we that we are in him.

6. He that saith he abideth in him ought himself also so to walk, even as he walked.— 1 *John* 2.

12. And I saw the dead, small and great, stand before God; and the books were opened: and another book was opened, which is the book of life: and the dead were judged out of those things which were written in the books, according to their works.—*Rev.* 20.

14. Blessed are they that do his commandments, that they may have right to the tree of life, and may enter in through the gates into the city.—*Rev.* 22.

REPENTANCE.

THE SECOND PRINCIPLE OF THE GOSPEL.

1. In those days came John the Baptist, *Preached* preaching in the wilderness of Judæa. *by John th Baptist:*

2. And saying, Repent ye: for the kingdom of heaven is at hand.—*Matt.* 3.

14. Now after that John was put in prison, *By the* Jesus came into Galilee, preaching the gospel *Savior:* of the kingdom of God,

15. And saying, The time is fulfilled, and the kingdom of God is at hand: repent ye, and believe the gospel.—*Mark.* 1.

7. And he called unto him the twelve, and *By the* began to send them forth by two and two; and *Apostles:* gave them power over unclean spirits;

12. And they went out, and preached that men should repent.—*Mark* 6.

38. Then Peter said unto them, Repent, and *By Peter:* be baptized every one of you in the name of Jesus Christ for the remission of sins, and ye shall receive the gift of the Holy Ghost.—*Acts* 2.

19. Repent ye therefore, and be converted, that your sins may be blotted out, when the times of refreshing shall come from the presence of the Lord.—*Acts* 3.

30. And the times of this ignorance God *By Paul:* winked at; but now commandeth all men everywhere to repent.—*Acts* 17.

19. Whereupon, O king Agrippa, I was not disobedient unto the heavenly vision:

20. But showed first unto them of Damascus, and at Jerusalem, and throughout all the coasts of Judæa, and then to the Gentiles, that they should repent and turn to God, and do works meet for repentance.—*Acts* 26.

Commanded   19. As many as I love, I rebuke and chasten: be zealous therefore, and repent.—*Rev.* 3.

Necessity of Repentance: 20. Then began he to upbraid the cities wherein most of his mighty works were done, because they repented not:

21. Woe unto thee, Chorazin! woe unto thee, Bethsaida! for if the mighty works, which were done in you, had been done in Tyre and Sidon, they would have repented long ago in sackcloth and ashes.

22. But I say unto you, It shall be more tolerable for Tyre and Sidon at the day of judgment than for you.—*Matt.* 11.

31. * * * Jesus saith unto them, Verily I say unto you, that the publicans and harlots go into the kingdom of God before you.

32. For John came unto you in the way of righteousness, and ye believed him not: but the publicans and the harlots believed him: and ye, when ye had seen it, repented not afterward, that ye might believe him.—*Matt.* 21.

Two kinds of Repentance: 9. Now I rejoice, not that ye were made sorry, but that ye sorrowed to repentance: for ye were made sorry after a godly manner, that ye might receive damage by us in nothing.

10. For godly sorrow worketh repentance to salvation not to be repented of: but the sorrow of the world worketh death.—2 *Cor.* 7.

Acceptable kind: 7. But when he saw many of the Pharisees and Sadducees come to his baptism, he said unto them, O generation of vipers, who hath warned you to flee from the wrath to come?

8. Bring forth therefore fruits meet for repentance:

9. And think not to say within yourselves, We have Abraham to our Father: for I say unto you, that God is able of these stones to raise up children unto Abraham.—*Matt.* 3.

⌒ 25. Wherefore putting away lying, speak *Acceptable kind:* every man truth with his neighbor: for we are members one of another.

26. Be ye angry, and sin not: let not the sun go down upon your wrath:

27. Neither give place to the devil.

28. Let him that stole steal no more: but rather let him labor, working with his hands the thing which is good, that he may have to give to him that needeth.--*Eph.* 4.

29. Let no corrupt communication proceed out of your mouth, but that which is good to the use of edifying, that it may minister grace unto the hearers.

30. And grieve not the Holy Spirit of God, whereby ye are sealed unto the day of redemption.

31. Let all bitterness, and wrath, and anger, and clamor, and evil speaking, be put away from you, with all malice:

32. And be ye kind one to another, tender-hearted, forgiving one another, even as God for Christ's sake hath forgiven you.—*Eph.* 4.

12. Therefore also now, saith the Lord, turn ye even to me with all your heart, and with fasting, and with weeping, and with mourning:

13. And rend your heart, and not your garments, and turn unto the Lord your God: for he is gracious and merciful, slow to anger, and of great kindness, and repenteth him of the evil.—*Joel* 2.

6. Seek ye the Lord while he may be found, call ye upon him while he is near:

7. Let the wicked forsake his way, and the unrighteous man his thoughts: and let him return unto the Lord, and he will have mercy upon him; and to our God, for he will abundantly pardon.—*Isa.* 55.

Acceptable kind: 24. And the servant of the Lord must not strive; but be gentle unto all men, apt to teach, patient;

25. In meekness instructing those that oppose themselves; if God peradventure will give them repentance to the acknowledging of the truth.—*2 Tim.* 2.

Rewards Promised: 7. At what instant I shall speak concerning a nation, and concerning a kingdom, to pluck up, and to pull down, and to destroy it;

8. If that nation, against whom I have pronounced, turn from their evil, I will repent of the evil that I thought to do unto them.—*Jer.* 18.

14. Again, when I say unto the wicked, Thou shalt surely die; if he turn from his sin, and do that which is lawful and right;

15. If the wicked restore the pledge, give again that he had robbed, walk in the statutes of life, without committing iniquity; he shall surely live, he shall not die.

16. None of his sins that he hath committed shall be mentioned unto him: he hath done that which is lawful and right; he shall surely live.—*Ezek.* 33.

Penalty of non-repentance: 41. The men of Nineveh shall rise in judgment with this generation, and shall condemn it: because they repented at the preaching of Jonas: and, behold, a greater than Jonas is here.—*Matt.* 12.

20. Notwithstanding I have a few things against thee, because thou sufferest that woman Jezebel, which calleth herself a prophetess, to teach and to seduce my servants to commit fornication, and to eat things sacrificed unto idols.

21. And I gave her space to repent of her fornication; and she repented not.—*Rev.* 2.

22. Behold, I will cast her into a bed, and *Penalty of non-repentance:* them that commit adultery with her into great tribulation, except they repent of their deeds. —*Rev.* 2.

4. Or those eighteen, upon whom the tower in Siloam fell, and slew them, think ye that they were sinners above all men that dwelt in Jerusalem?

5. I tell you, nay: but, except ye repent, ye shall all likewise perish.—*Luke* 13.

19. Now the works of the flesh are manifest, *Sins to be Repented of:* which are these; Adultery, fornication, uncleanness, lasciviousness,

20. Idolatry, witchcraft, hatred, variance, emulations., wrath, strife, seditions, heresies,

21. Envyings, murders, drunkenness, revellings, and such like: of the which I tell you before, as I have also told you in time past, that they which do such things shall not inherit the kingdom of God.—*Gal.* 5.

3. But fornication, and all uncleanness, or covetousness, let it not be once named among you, as becometh saints;

4. Neither filthiness, nor foolish talking, nor jesting, which are not convenient: but rather giving of thanks.

5. For this ye know, that no whoremonger, nor unclean person, nor covetous man, who is an idolater, hath any inheritance in the kingdom of Christ and of God.

6. Let no man deceive you with vain words: for because of these things cometh the wrath of God upon the children of disobedience.— *Eph.* 5.

11. For the grace of God that bringeth salvation hath appeared to all men.—*Titus* 2.

Sins to be Repented of: 12. Teaching us, that denying ungodliness, and worldly lusts, we should live soberly, righteously, and godly, in this present world.--*Titus* 2.

Should be Universal: 45. Then opened he their understanding, that they might understand the scriptures,

46. And said unto them, Thus it is written, and thus it behooved Christ to suffer, and to rise from the dead the third day:

47. And that repentance and remission of sins should be preached in his name among all nations, beginning at Jerusalem.—*Luke* 24.

18. When they heard these things, they held their peace, and glorified God, saying, Then hath God also to the Gentiles granted repentance unto life.—*Acts* 11.

9. The Lord is not slack concerning his promise, as some men count slackness; but is longsuffering to us-ward, not willing that any should perish, but that all should come to repentance.—*2 Pet.* 3.

30. And the times of this ignorance God winked at; but now commandeth all men everywhere to repent.—*Acts* 17.

A cause of joy in Heaven: 7. I say unto you, that likewise joy shall be in heaven over one sinner that repenteth, more than over ninety and nine just persons, which need no repentance. —*Luke* 15.

All Sinful: 8. If we say that we have no sin, we deceive ourselves, and the truth is not in us.

9. If we confess our sins, he is faithful and just to forgive us our sins, and to cleanse us from all unrighteousness.—1 *John* 1.

10. As it is written, there is none righteous, no, not one.—*Rom.* 3.

20. For there is not a just man upon earth, that doeth good, and sinneth not.—*Eccl.* 7.

BAPTISM.

THE THIRD PRINCIPLE OF THE GOSPEL.

15. And he said unto them, Go ye into all *A law*
the world, and preach the gospel to every *of God:*
creature.

16. He that believeth and is baptized shall
be saved; but he that believeth not shall be
damned.—*Mark* 16.

19. Go ye therefore, and teach all nations,
baptizing them in the name of the Father, and
of the Son, and of the Holy Ghost;

20. Teaching them to observe all things
whatsoever I have commanded you: and, lo, I
am with you alway, even unto the end of the
world Amen.—*Matt.* 28.

13. Then cometh Jesus from Galilee to Jor- *That even*
dan unto John, to be baptized of him. *Jesus must obey:*

14. But John forbade him, saying, I have
need to be baptized of thee, and comest thou to
me?

15. And Jesus answering said unto him,
Suffer it to be so now: for thus it becometh us
to fulfill all righteousness. Then he suffered
him.—*Matt.* 3.

29. And all the people that heard him, and *The counsel*
the publicans, justified God, being baptized *of God:*
with the baptism of John.

30. But the Pharisees and lawyers rejected
the counsel of God against themselves, being
not baptized of him. —*Luke* 7.

5. Jesus answered, Verily, verily, I say unto *Essential to*
thee, Except a man be born of water and of *salvation:*
the Spirit, he cannot enter into the kingdom of
God.—*John* 3.

Essential to salvation: 1. There was a certain man in Cæsarea called Cornelius, a centurion of the band called the Italian band,

2. A devout man, and one that feared God with all his house, which gave much alms to the people, and prayed to God alway.

3. He saw in a vision evidently about the ninth hour of the day an angel of God coming in to him, and saying unto him, Cornelius.

4. And when he looked on him, he was afraid, and said, What is it, Lord? And he said unto him, Thy prayers and thine alms are come up for a memorial before God.

5. And now send men to Joppa, and call for one Simon, whose surname is Peter:

6. He lodgeth with one Simon a tanner, whose house is by the sea side: he shall tell thee what thou oughtest to do.—*Acts* 10.

14. Who shall tell thee words whereby thou and all thy house shall be saved.—*Acts* 11.

Peter's command: 48. And he commanded them to be baptized in the name of the Lord: Then prayed they him to tarry certain days.—*Acts* 10.

Baptism of the Jailor: 30. And brought them out, and said, Sirs, what must I do to be saved?

31. And they said, Believe on the Lord Jesus Christ, and thou shalt be saved, and thy house.

32. And they spake unto him the word of the Lord, and to all that were in his house.

33. And he took them the same hour of the night, and washed their stripes; and was baptized, he and all his, straightway.—*Acts* 16.

26. For ye are all the children of God by faith in Christ Jesus.

27. For as many of you as have been baptized into Christ have put on Christ.—*Gal.* 3.

21. The like figure whereunto, even baptism, doth also now save us,(not the putting away of the filth of the flesh, but the answer of a good conscience toward God,) by the resurrection of Jesus Christ.—I *Pet.* 3.

MODE OF BAPTISM.

NOTE.—The word baptize is from the Greek *baptizo* or *bapto*, signifying to dip, plunge or immerse. Such classical writers as Polybius, Strabo, and Dion Cassius, who lived prior to or at the time of the Savior, used the word in this sense, from which it is fair to infer that such was the meaning intended where it is used in the New Testament. Not only do the most learned authors and linguists, ancient and modern, agree as to the definition here given, but a great many of the early "Christian Fathers," historians and commentators give us their testimony that baptism by immersion was practiced in the primitive Christian church. (See "Testimonies of Ancient and Modern Authors in Relation to Baptism," Vols. 21 and 22 *Millennial Star.*)

Mosheim, in his "Ecclesiastical History," Vol. I, page 129, says: "The sacrament of baptism was administered in this [first] century without the public assemblies, in places appointed and prepared for that purpose, and was performed by immersion of the whole body in the baptismal font." Again (page 211) he says: "The persons [in the second century] that were to be baptized * * * were immersed under water, and received into Christ's kingdom by a solemn invocation of Father, Son and Holy Ghost, according to the expressed command of our blessed Lord."

Martin Luther says: "The term baptism is a Greek word: it may be rendered by dipping as when we dip anything in water that it may be entirely covered with water. I could wish that such as are to be baptized should be completely immersed into water according to the meaning of the word and the signification of the ordinance; not because I think it necessary, but it would be beautiful to have a full and perfect sign of so perfect and full a thing; as also, without doubt, it was instituted by Christ."

Calvin says: "The word baptize signifies to immerse and the rite of immersion was observed by the ancient Church."

Bossuet, the celebrated French bishop, says; "We are able to make it appear, by the acts of Councils and by the ancient rituals, that for thirteen hundred years baptism was thus [by immersion] administered throughout the whole church as far as possible."

Schaff, an ancient Swiss theologian, says: "As to the outward mode of administering this [baptismal] ordinance, immersion, and not sprinkling, was unquestionably the original, normal form. * * * Not till the end of the 13th century did sprinkling become the rule, and immersion the exception."

Baxter, the great non-conformist, says: "We grant that baptism, then (in the primitive times), was by washing the whole body. Though we have thought it lawful to disuse the manner of dipping, and to use less water, yet we presume not to change the use and signification of it."

John Wesley writes: "'Buried with him'—alluding to the ancient manner of baptizing by immersion."

Jeremy Taylor, the learned bishop, writes: "The custom of the ancient churches was not sprinkling, but immersion, in pursuance of the sense of the word in the commandment and the example of our blessed Savior."

Robinson, the great philologist, and biblical scholar, says: "The native Greeks must understand their own language better than foreigners, and they have always understood the word baptism to signify dipping; and therefore from their first embracing of Christianity to this day, they have always baptized and do yet baptize by immersion."

Proofs in favor of Immersion: 16. And Jesus, when he was baptized, went up straightway out of the water: and, lo, the heavens were opened unto him, and he saw the Spirit of God descending like a dove, and lighting upon him.—*Matt.* 3.

5. And there went out unto him all the land of Judæa, and they of Jerusalem, and were all baptized of him in the river of Jordan, confessing their sins.

9. And it came to pass in those days, that Jesus came from Nazareth of Galilee, and was baptized of John in Jordan.

10. And straightway coming up out of the water, he saw the heavens opened, and the Spirit like a dove descending upon him.—*Mark* 1.

23. And John also was baptizing in Ænon near to Salim, because there was much water there: and they came, and were baptized.—*John* 3.

38. And he commanded the chariot to stand still: and they went down both into the water, both Philip and the eunuch; and he baptized him.—*Acts* 8.

39. And when they were come up out of the *Proofs in* water, the Spirit of the Lord caught away *favor of* Philip, that the eunuch saw him no more: and *immersion*· he went on his way rejoicing.—*Acts* 8.

3. Know ye not, that so many of us as were baptized into Jesus Christ were baptized into his death?

4. Therefore we are buried with him by bap- *Compared to* tism into death: that like as Christ was raised *a burial.* up from the dead by the glory of the Father, even so we also should walk in newness of life.

5. For if we have been planted together in *Compared to* the likeness of his death, we shall be also in *a planting:* the likeness of his resurrection.—*Rom.* 6.

12. Buried with him in baptism, wherein also ye are risen with him through the faith of the operation of God, who hath raised him from the dead.—*Col.* 2.

33. And he took them the same hour of the *Not baptized* night, and washed their stripes; and was bap- *in the house,* tized, he and all his, straightway. *though at*
night:
34. And when he had brought them into his house, he set meat before them, and rejoiced, believing in God with all his house.—*Acts.* 16.

OBJECT OF BAPTISM.

4. John did baptize in the wilderness, and *For the* preach the baptism of repentance for the remis- *remission of* sion of sins.—*Mark* 1. *sins:*

3. And he came into all the country about Jordan, preaching the baptism of repentance for the remission of sins.—*Luke* 3.

38. Then Peter said unto them, Repent, and be baptized every one of you in the name of Jesus Christ for the remission of sins, and ye shall receive the gift of the Holy Ghost.—*Acts* 2.

For the remission of sins:

41. Then they that gladly received his word were baptized: and the same day there were added unto them about three thousand souls. —*Acts* 2.

16. And now why tarriest thou? arise, and be baptized, and wash away thy sins, calling on the name of the Lord.—*Acts* 22.

PROPER SUBJECTS FOR BAPTISM.

Must be capable of being taught

19. Go ye therefore, and teach all nations, baptizing them in the name of the Father, and of the Son, and of the Holy Ghost:

20. Teaching them to observe all things whatsoever I have commanded you: and, lo, I am with you alway, even unto the end of the world. Amen.—*Matt.* 28.

And of believing:

16. He that believeth and is baptized shall be saved; but he that believeth not shall be damned.—*Mark* 16.

12. But when they believed Philip preaching the things concerning the kingdom of God, and the name of Jesus Christ, they were baptized, both men and women.

36. And as they went on their way, they came unto a certain water: and the eunuch said, See, here is water; what doth hinder me to be baptized?

37. And Philip said, If thou believest with all thine heart, thou mayest. And he answered and said, I believe that Jesus Christ is the Son of God.—*Acts* 8.

34. Then Peter opened his mouth, and said, Of a truth I perceive that God is no respecter of persons:

35. But in every nation he that feareth him, and worketh righteousness, is accepted with him.—*Acts* 10.

43. To him give all the prophets witness, *And of* that through his name whosoever believeth in *believing:* him shall receive remission of sins.

48. And he commanded them to be baptized in the name of the Lord. Then prayed they him to tarry certain days.—*Acts* 10.

32. And they spake unto him the word of the Lord, and to all that were in his house.

33. And he took them the same hour of the night, and washed their stripes; and was baptized, he and all his, straightway.

34. And when he had brought them into his house, he set meat before them, and rejoiced, believing in God with all his house.—*Acts* 16.

8. And Crispus, the chief ruler of the synagogue, believed on the Lord with all his house; and many of the Corinthians hearing believed, and were baptized.—*Acts* 18.

38. Then Peter said unto them, Repent, and *Must be* be baptized every one of you in the name of *capable of* Jesus Christ for the remission of sins, and ye *repenting:* shall receive the gift of the Holy Ghost.

39. For the promise is unto you, and to your children, and to all that are afar off, even as many as the Lord our God shall call.

40. And with many other words did he testify and exhort, saying, Save yourselves from this untoward generation.

41. Then they that gladly received his word *Must be cap-* were baptized: and the same day there were *able of receiv-* added unto them about three thousand souls. *ing the word:* —*Acts* 2.

7. Then said he to the multitude that came forth to be baptized of him, O generation of vipers, who hath warned you to flee from the wrath to come?—*Luke* 3.

And bring-
ing forth
fruits:

8. Bring forth therefore fruits worthy of repentance, and begin not to say within yourselves, We have Abraham to our father: for I say unto you, That God is able of these stones to raise up children unto Abraham.—*Luke* 3.

32. I came not to call the righteous, but sinners to repentance.—*Luke* 5.

Little chil-
dren have no
sin to re-
pent of:

13. And they brought young children to him, that he should touch them: and his disciples rebuked those that brought them.

14. But when Jesus saw it, he was much displeased, and said unto them, Suffer the little children to come unto me, and forbid them not: for of such is the kingdom of God.

15. Verily I say unto you, Whosoever shall not receive the kingdom of God as a little child, he shall not enter therein.

16. And he took them up in his arms, put his hands upon them, and blessed them.—*Mark* 10.

16. And I baptized also the household of Stephanas: besides, I know not whether I baptized any other.—1 *Cor.* 1.

15. I beseech you, brethren, (ye know the house of Stephanas, that it is the first-fruits of Achaia, and that they have addicted themselves to the ministry of the saints.)

16. That ye submit yourselves unto such, and to everyone that helpeth with us, and laboreth.—1 *Cor.* 16.

NOTE.—The baptizing or sprinkling of infants is a man-made doctrine, for which there is no warrant in the Scriptures. The advocates of infant baptism frequently quote 1 Cor. i, 16 (as given above), in support of their theory, but the reference to Stephanas in 1 Cor. xvi, 15, 16,(which see also above), proves that his family consisted of adults.

Tertullian, one of the Latin Fathers, wrote: "Let them therefore come when they are grown up—when they can understand—when they are taught whither they are to come. Let them become Christians when they can know Christ. Why should this innocent age hasten to the remission of sins? * * * If persons understand the importance of baptism, they will rather fear the consequent obligation than the delay."

Calvin says: "But as Christ enjoins them [in Mark xvi, 16] to teach before baptizing, and desires that none but believers shall be admitted to baptism, it would appear that baptism is not properly administered unless when it is preceded by faith. * * * [In] the Apostolic age * * * no one is found to have been admitted to baptism without a previous profession of faith and repentance."

Curcellæus writes: "The baptism of infants in the two first centuries after Christ was altogether unknown. * * * The custom of baptizing infants did not begin before the third age after Christ was born. In the former ages no trace of it appears; and it was introduced without the command of Christ.

Dr. Neander, the great German scholar, says: "It is certain that Christ did not ordain infant baptism. * * * We cannot prove that the Apostles ordained infant baptism. From those places where the baptism of a whole family is mentioned, as in Acts xvi, 33, 1 Cor. i, 16, we can draw no such conclusion, because the inquiry is still to be made whether there were any children in these famlies of such an age that they were not capable of any intelligent reception of Christianity, for this is the only point on which the case turns. * * * That not till so late a period as (at least certainly not earlier than) Irenæus, a trace of infant baptism appears; and that it first became recognized as an apostolic tradition in the course of the third century, is evidence rather *against* than *for* the admission of its apostolic origin."

Bishop Jeremy Taylor says:"From the action of Christ's blessing infants, to infer they are to be baptized, proves nothing so much as that there is a want of better argument; for the conclusion would with more probability be derived thus: Christ blessed infants, and so dismissed them; but baptized them not; therefore infants are not to be baptized."

Martin Luther says: "It cannot be proved by the sacred Scriptures that infant baptism was instituted by Christ, or begun by the first Christians after the Apostles."

The first case of which we find any record wherein the form of baptism was changed was that of Novatian, who lived during the third century. Gahan, a Catholic historian, writing of him, says: "Having embraced the faith, he continued a catechumen, till, falling dangerously ill, and his life being despaired of, he was baptized in bed, *not by immersion, which was then the usual method,* but by infusion, or pouring on of water. On recovering, he received not the seal of the Lord by the hand of the bishop, says St. Pacian, that is to say, the sacrament of confirmation. Both of these defects were, by the ancient discipline of the church, bars to holy orders."

THE HOLY GHOST.

THE CONFERRING OF WHICH CONSTITUTES THE FOURTH PRINCIPLE OF THE GOSPEL.

Promised by the Savior: 16. And I will pray the Father, and he shall give you another Comforter, that he may abide with you for ever.—*John* 14.

7. Nevertheless I tell you the truth; It is expedient for you that I go away: for if I go not away, the Comforter will not come unto you; but if I depart, I will send him unto you. —*John* 16.

49. And, behold, I send the promise of my Father unto you: but tarry ye in the city of Jerusalem, until ye be endued with power from on high.—*Luke* 24.

Promised by Peter: 38. Then Peter said unto them, Repent, and be baptized every one of you in the name of Jesus Christ for the remission of sins, and ye shall receive the gift of the Holy Ghost.— *Acts* 2.

What it should do: 26. But the Comforter, which is the Holy Ghost, whom the Father will send in my name, he shall teach you all things, and bring all things to your remembrance, whatsoever I have said unto you.—*John* 14.

26. But when the Comforter is come, whom I will send unto you from the Father, even the Spirit of truth, which proceedeth from the Father, he shall testify of me.—*John* 15.

13. Howbeit when he, the Spirit of truth, is come, he will guide you into all truth: for he shall not speak of himself; but whatsoever he shall hear, that shall he speak: and he will show you things to come.—*John* 16.

14. He shall glorify me: for he shall receive *What it* of mine, and shall show it unto you.—*John* 16. *should do:*

11. And when they bring you unto the synagogues, and unto magistrates, and powers, take ye no thought how or what thing ye shall answer, or what ye shall say:

12. For the Holy Ghost shall teach you in the same hour what ye ought to say.—*Luke* 12.

8. But ye shall receive power, after that the Holy Ghost is come upon you: and ye shall be witnesses unto me both in Jerusalem, and in all Judæa, and in Samaria, and unto the uttermost part of the earth.—*Acts* 1.

9. But as it is written, Eye hath not seen, nor ear heard, neither have entered into the heart of man, the things which God hath prepared for them that love him.

10. But God hath revealed them unto us by his Spirit: for the Spirit searcheth all things. yea, the deep things of God.

12. Now we have received, not the spirit of the world, but the Spirit which is of God; that we might know the things that are freely given to us of God.

13. Which things also we speak, not in the words which man's wisdom teacheth, but which the Holy Ghost teacheth; comparing spiritual things with spiritual.—1 *Cor.* 2.

20. But ye have an unction from the Holy One, and ye know all things.

27. But the anointing which ye have received of him abideth in you, and ye need not that any man teach you: but as the same anointing teacheth you of all things, and is truth, and is no lie, and even as it hath taught you, ye shall abide in him.—1 *John* 2.

What it should do: 16. The Spirit itself beareth witness with our spirit, that we are the children of God:— *Rom.* 8.

Manifestations of the Spirit: 4. Now there are diversities of gifts, but the same Spirit.

7. But the manifestation of the Spirit is given to every man to profit withal.

8. For to one is given by the Spirit the word of wisdom; to another the word of knowledge by the same Spirit:

9. To another faith by the same Spirit; to another the gifts of healing by the same Spirit;

10. To another the working of miracles; to another prophecy; to another discerning of spirits; to another divers kinds of tongues; to another the interpretation of tongues;

11. But all these worketh that one and the selfsame Spirit, dividing to every man severally as he will.

28. And God hath set some in the church, first apostles, secondarily prophets, thirdly teachers, after that miracles, then gifts of healings, helps, governments, diversities of tongues.

29. Are all apostles? are all prophets? are all teachers? are all workers of miracles?

30. Have all the gifts of healing? do all speak with tongues? do all interpret?—1 *Cor.* 12.

17. And these signs shall follow them that believe; In my name shall they cast out devils; they shall speak with new tongues;

18. They shall take up serpents; and if they drink any deadly thing, it shall not hurt them; they shall lay hands on the sick, and they shall recover.—*Mark* 16.

22. The fruit of the Spirit is love, joy, *Fruit of*
peace, long-suffering, gentleness, goodness, faith, *the Spirit:*

23. Meekness, temperance: against such
there is no law.—*Gal.* 5.

14. Now when the apostles which were at *How*
Jerusalem heard that Samaria had received the *conferred:*
word of God, they sent unto them Peter and
John:

15. Who, when they were come down, prayed
for them, that they might receive the Holy
Ghost:

16. (For as yet he was fallen upon none of
them: only they were baptized in the name of
the Lord Jesus.)   *Conferred by*

17. Then laid they their hands on them, and *the laying on*
they received the Holy Ghost. X   *of hands:*

18. And when Simon saw that through laying on of the apostles' hands the Holy Ghost X
was given, he offered them money,

19. Saying, Give me also this power, that on
whomsoever I lay hands, he may receive the
Holy Ghost.

20. But Peter said unto him, Thy money
perish with thee, because thou hast thought
that the gift of God may be purchased with
money.—*Acts* 8.

1. And it came to pass, that, while Apollos
was at Corinth, Paul having passed through
the upper coasts came to Ephesus: and finding
certain disciples,

2. He said unto them, Have ye received the
Holy Ghost since ye believed? And they said
unto him, We have not so much as heard
whether there be any Holy Ghost. X

3. And he said unto them, Unto what then
were ye baptized? And they said, Unto John's
baptism.—*Acts* 19.

Conferred by the laying on of hands: 4. Then said Paul, John verily baptized with the baptism of repentance, saying unto the people, that they should believe on him which should come after him, that is, on Christ Jesus.

5. When they heard this, they were baptized in the name of the Lord Jesus.

6. And when Paul had laid his hands upon them, the Holy Ghost came on them; and they spake with tongues, and prophesied.—*Acts* 19.

14. Neglect not the gift that is in thee, which was given thee by prophecy, with the laying on of the hands of the presbytery.—1 *Tim.* 4.

6. Wherefore I put thee in remembrance that thou stir up the gift of God, which is in thee by the putting on of my hands.—2 *Tim.* 1

1. Therefore leaving the principles of the doctrine of Christ, let us go on unto perfection; not laying again the foundation of repentance from dead works, and of faith toward God,

2. Of the doctrine of baptisms, and of laying on of hands, and of resurrection of the dead, and of eternal judgment.—*Heb.* 6.

NOTE.—There is ample proof in the writings of ancient historians that the Holy Ghost was conferred upon baptized believers in the primitive church by prayer and the laying on of hands, and that this rite or ordinance was practiced in the Christian churches for a considerable period after the days of the apostles.

Tertullian, one of the Latin Fathers, writing in the second century, says: "After baptism succeeds the *laying on of hands*, with prayer, calling for the Holy Ghost."

Cyprian, a writer of the third century, says: "Our practice is, that those who have been baptized into the church should be presented, that by prayer and *imposition of hands* they may receive the Holy Ghost." Again he says: "It is manifest where, and by whom the remission of sins, which is conferred in baptism, is administered. They who are presented to the rulers of the church, obtain, *by our prayers and imposition of hands*, the Holy Ghost."

Mosheim, the great German historian, writing of the third century, says: "This ceremony [that of baptism] was performed only in the presence of such as were already initiated into the Christian mysteries. The remission of sins was thought to be its immediate and happy fruit, while the bishop, *by prayer and the imposition of hands*, was supposed to confer those sanctifying gifts of the Holy Ghost, that are necessary to a life of righteousness and virtue."

Eusebius, in his Ecclesiastical History (page 113), alludes to this ordinance, in referring to the baptism of Novatian, as follows: "He * * * fell into a grievous distemper, and it being supposed that he would die immediately, he received baptism (being besprinkled with water) on the bed where he lay (if that can be termed baptism): neither when he had escaped that sickness, did he afterwards receive the other things which the canon of the church enjoineth should be received: nor was he sealed by the bishop's imposition of hands; which if he never received, how did he receive the Holy Ghost?"

Augustine, in the fourth century, says: "We still do what the apostles did when they *laid their hands* on the Samaritans and called down the Holy Ghost upon them."

LAYING ON OF HANDS FOR THE HEALING OF THE SICK.

NOTE.—The ordinance of laying on hands with prayer is used in other cases as well as in that of confirming a person a member of the Church and conferring the Holy Ghost; as, for instance, for the healing of the sick, bestowing patriarchal or other blessings, and for ordination (See Divine Authority).

Cases of healing under the Savior's hands:

18. While he spake these things unto them, behold, there came a certain ruler, and worshiped him, saying, My daughter is even now dead: but come and lay thy hand upon her, and she shall live.—*Matt.* 9.

5. And he could there do no mighty work, save that he laid his hands upon a few sick folk, and healed them.—*Mark* 6.

40. Now when the sun was setting, all they that had any sick with divers diseases brought them unto him; and he laid his hands on every one of them, and healed them.—*Luke* 4.

11. And, behold, there was a woman which had a spirit of infirmity eighteen years, and was bowed together, and could in nowise lift up herself.—*Luke* 13.

Cases of heal-
ing under
the Savior's
hands.

12. And when Jesus saw her, he called her to him, and said unto her, Woman, thou art loosed from thine infirmity.

13. And he laid his hands on her: and immediately she was made straight, and glorified God.—*Luke* 13.

23. And he took the blind man by the hand, and led him out of town; and when he had spit on his eyes, and put his hands upon him, he asked him if he saw aught.

24. And he looked up, and said, I see men as trees, walking.

25. After that he put his hands upon his eyes, and made him look up: and he was restored, and saw every man clearly.—*Mark 8.*

30. And, behold, two blind men sitting by the way side, when they heard that Jesus passed by, cried out, saying, Have mercy on us, O Lord, thou son of David.

34. So Jesus had compassion on them, and touched their eyes: and immediately their eyes received sight, and they followed him.— *Matt.* 20.

Power to heal
promised:

18. They shall take up serpents; and if they drink any deadly thing it shall not hurt them; they shall lay hands on the sick, and they shall recover.—*Mark* 16.

1. And when he had called unto him his twelve disciples, he gave them power against unclean spirits, to cast them out, and to heal all manner of sickness and all manner of disease. —*Matt.* 10.

13. And they cast out many devils, and anointed with oil many that were sick, and healed them.—*Mark* 6.

14. Is any sick among you? let him call for *Advice of* the Elders of the church; and let them pray *James:* over him, anointing him with oil in the name of the Lord:

15. And the prayer of faith shall save the sick, and the Lord shall raise him up; and if he have committed sin, they shall be forgiven him.—*Jas.* 5.

17. And Ananias went his way, and entered *Healing un-* into the house; and putting his hands on him *der the hands* said, Brother Saul, the Lord, even Jesus, that *of Ananias:* appeared unto thee in the way as thou camest, hath sent me that thou mightest receive thy sight, and be filled with the Holy Ghost.— *Acts* 9.

8. And it came to pass, that the father of *And Paul:* Publius lay sick of a fever and of a bloody flux: to whom Paul entered in, and prayed, and laid his hands on him, and healed him.—*Acts* 28.

LAYING ON OF HANDS TO CONFER BLESSINGS.

14. And Israel stretched out his right hand, and laid it upon Ephraim's head, who was the younger, and his left hand upon Manasseh's head, guiding his hand wittingly; for Manasseh was the first born.—*Gen.* 48.

13. And they brought young children to him, that he should touch them; and his disciples rebuked those that brought them.

14. But when Jesus saw it, he was much displeased, and said unto them, Suffer the little children to come unto me, and forbid them not: for of such is the kingdom of God.

15. Verily I say unto you, Whosoever shall not receive the kingdom of God as a little child, he shall not enter therein.

16. And he took them up in his arms, put his hands upon them, and blessed them.— *Mark* 10.

CHURCH ORGANIZATION.

WHAT THE CHURCH OF CHRIST CONSISTS OF, AND HOW IT MAY BE KNOWN.

NOTE.—The Church of Christ was an organization which the Savior established among men while He dwelt upon the earth, and which consisted of certain officers as well as members, who possessed various gifts and powers obtained from a divine source, which distinguished the Church from every other organization in existence. To become members of the Church of Christ, persons were required to accept the Gospel, and to conform to its requirements.

Officers of the Church:

27. Now ye are the body of Christ, and members in particular.

28. And God hath set some in the church, first apostles, secondarily prophets, thirdly teachers, after that miracles, then gifts of healings, helps, governments, diversities of tongues.

29. Are all apostles? are all prophets? are all teachers? are all workers of miracles?

30. Have all the gifts of healing? do all speak with tongues? do all interpret?

31. But covet earnestly the best gifts: and yet show I unto you a more excellent way.— 1 *Cor.* 12.

19. Now therefore ye are no more strangers and foreigners, but fellow citizens with the saints, and of the household of God;

20. And are built upon the foundation of the apostles and prophets, Jesus Christ himself being the chief corner stone;

21. In whom all the building fitly framed together groweth unto an holy temple in the Lord.—*Eph.* 2.

8. Wherefore, he saith, When he ascended up on high, he led captivity captive, and gave gifts unto men.—*Eph.* 4.

11. And he gave some, apostles; and some, *Officers of* prophets ; and some, evangelists; and some, *the Church:* pastors and teachers;

12. For the perfecting of the saints, for the *Why placed* work of the ministry, for the edifying of the *in the Church:* body of Christ:

13. Till we all come in the unity of the *How long to* faith, and of the knowledge of the Son of God, *continue:* unto a perfect man, unto the measure of the stature of the fulness of Christ;

14. That we henceforth be no more children, tossed to and fro, and carried about with every wind of doctrine, by the sleight of men, and cunning craftiness, whereby they lie in wait to deceive;

15. But speaking the truth in love, may grow up into him in all things, which is the head, even Christ.

16. From whom the whole body fitly joined together and compacted by that which every joint supplieth, according to the effectual working in the measure of every part, maketh increase of the body unto the edifying of itself in love.—*Eph.* 4.

9. (Beforetime in Israel, when a man went *Prophets* to inquire of God, thus he spake, Come, and *and Apostles* let us go to the seer: for he that is now called a Prophet was beforetime called a Seer.)— 1 *Sam.* 9.

13. And by a prophet the Lord brought Israel out of Egypt, and by a prophet was he preserved.—*Hos.* 12.

11. And the multitude said, This is Jesus the prophet of Nazareth of Galilee.—*Matt.* 21.

13. And when it was day, he called unto him his disciples: and of them he chose twelve, whom also he named apostles.—*Luke* 6.

5

Prophets
and Apostles

28. For I say unto you, Among those that are born of women there is not a greater prophet than John the Baptist: but he that is least in the kingdom of God is greater than he.—*Luke* 7.

49. Therefore also said the wisdom of God, I will send them prophets and apostles, and some of them they shall slay and persecute:

50. That the blood of all the prophets, which was shed from the foundation of the world, may be required of this generation.—*Luke* 11.

22. For Moses truly said unto the fathers, A prophet shall the Lord your God raise up unto you of your brethren, like unto me; him shall ye hear in all things whatsoever he shall say unto you.

23. And it shall come to pass that every soul, which will not hear that prophet, shall be destroyed from among the people.

24. Yea, and all the prophets from Samuel and those that follow after, as many as have spoken, have likewise foretold of these days.—*Acts* 3.

1. Paul, an apostle, (not of men, neither by man, but by Jesus Christ, and God the Father, who raised him from the dead.)—*Gal.* 1.

19. Now therefore ye are no more strangers and foreigners, but fellowcitizens with the saints, and of the household of God;

20. And are built upon the foundation of the apostles and prophets, Jesus Christ himself being the chief corner stone;

21. In whom all the building fitly framed together groweth unto an holy temple in the Lord.—*Eph.* 2

3. How that by revelation he made known *Prophets* unto me the mystery; (as I wrote afore in few *and Apostles* words,

4. Whereby, when ye. read, ye may understand my knowledge in the mystery of Christ.)

5. Which in other ages was not made known · unto the sons of men, as it is now revealed unto his holy apostles and prophets by the Spirit.—*Eph.* 3.

1. Wherefore, holy brethren, partakers of the heavenly calling, consider the Apostle and High Priest of our profession, Christ Jesus;
2. Who was faithful to him that appointed him, as also Moses was faithful in all his house.—*Heb.* 3.

10. And as we tarried there many days, there came down from Judæa a certain prophet named Agabus.—*Acts* 21.

8. And the next day we that were of Paul's *Evangelists:* company departed, and came unto Cæsarea: and we entered into the house of Philip the evangelist, which was one of the seven; and abode with him.—*Acts* 21.

5. But watch thou in all things, endure afflictions, do the work of an evangelist, make full proof of thy mystery.—2 *Tim.* 4.

1. Wherefore, holy brethren, partakers of *High Priests* the heavenly calling, consider the Apostle and High Priest of our profession, Christ Jesus.— *Heb.* 3.

14. Seeing that we have a great High Priest that is passed into the heavens, Jesus the Son of God, let us hold fast our profession.— *Heb.* 4.

High Priests   1. For every high priest taken from among men is ordained for men in things pertaining to God, that he may offer both gifts and sacrifices for sins.

10. Called of God an high priest after the order of Melchisedec.—*Heb.* 5.

1. Now the things which we have spoken this is the sum: We have such an High Priest, who is set on the right hand of the throne of the majesty in the heavens.—*Heb.* 8.

Seventies: 16. And the Lord said unto Moses, gather unto me seventy men of the elders of Israel, whom thou knowest to be the elders of the people, and officers over them; and bring them unto the tabernacle of the congregation, that they may stand there with thee.

17. And I will come down and talk with thee there: and I will take of the spirit which is upon thee, and will put it upon them; and they shall bear the burden of the people with thee, that thou bear it not thyself alone.

24. And Moses went out, and told the people the words of the Lord, and gathered the seventy men of the elders of the people, and set them round about the tabernacle.

25. And the Lord came down in a cloud, and spake unto him, and took of the spirit that was upon him, and gave it unto the seventy elders: and it came to pass, that, when the spirit rested upon them, they prophecied, and did not cease.—*Num.* 11.

1. After these things the Lord appointed other seventy also, and sent them two and two before his face into every city and place, whither he himself would come.

17. And the seventy returned again with joy, saying, Lord, even the devils are subject unto us through thy name.—*Luke* 10.

1. Paul and Timotheus, the servants of Jesus Christ, to all the saints in Christ Jesus which are at Philippi, with the bishops and deacons.— *Phili.* 1.

Bishops:

1. This is a true saying, If a man desire the office of a bishop, he desireth a good work.— 1 *Tim.* 3.

7. For a bishop must be blameless, as the steward of God; not selfwilled, not soon angry. not given to wine, no striker, not given to filthy lucre.—*Titus* 1.

23. And when they had ordained them elders in every church, and had prayed with fasting, they commended them to the Lord, on whom they believed.—*Acts* 14.

Elders:

6. And the apostles and elders came together for to consider of this matter—*Acts* 15.

17. Let the elders that rule well be counted worthy of double honor, especially they who labored in the word and doctrine.—1 *Tim.* 5.

1. The elders which are among you I exhort, who am also an elder, and witness of the sufferings of Christ, and also a partaker of the glory that shall be revealed:
.2. Feed the flock of God which is among you, taking the oversight thereof, not by constraint, but willingly; not for filthy lucre, but of a ready mind;
3. Neither as being lords over God's heritage, but being ensamples to the flock.— 1 *Pet.* 5.

5. There was in the days of Herod, the king of Judæa, a certain priest named Zacharias, of the course of Abia: and his wife was of the daughters of Aaron, and her name was Elizabeth.— *Luke* 1.

Priests:

Priests: 10. And hast made us unto our God kings and priests: and we shall reign on the earth.—*Rev.* 5.

6. Blessed and holy is he that hath part in the first resurrection: on such the second death hath no power, but they shall be priests of God and of Christ, and shall reign with him a thousand years.—*Rev.* 20.

Teachers: 1. Now there was in the church that was at Antioch certain prophets and teachers; as Barnabas, and Simeon that was called Niger, and Lucius of Cyrene, and Manaen, which had been brought up with Herod the tetrarch, and Saul.—*Acts* 13.

Deacons: 8. Likewise must the deacons be grave, not double-tongued, not given to much wine, not greedy of filthy lucre.

9. Holding the mystery of the faith in a pure conscience.

10. And let these also first be proved; then let them use the office of a deacon, being found blameless.

11. Even so must their wives be grave, not slanderers, sober, faithful in all things.

12. Let the deacons be the husbands of one wife, ruling their children and their own houses well.—1 *Tim.* 3.

1. Paul and Timotheus, the servants of Jesus Christ, to all the saints in Christ Jesus which are at Philippi, with the bishops and deacons.—*Phili.* 1.

Spiritual Gifts: 11. For I long to see you, that I may impart unto you some spiritual gift, to the end ye may be established.—*Rom.* 1.

8. Charity never faileth: but whether there be prophecies, they shall fail; whether there be tongues, they shall cease; whether there be knowledge, it shall vanish away.—1 *Cor.* 13.

9. For we know in part, and we prophecy in part.

Spiritual Gifts

10. But when that which is perfect shall come, then that which is in part shall be done away.

11. When I was a child, I spake as a child, I understood as a child, I thought as a child: but when I became a man, I put away childish things.

12. For now we see through a glass, darkly; but then face to face: now I know in part; but then shall I know even as I am known.

13. And now abideth faith, hope, charity, these three; but the greatest of these is charity, —1 *Cor.* 13.

1. Follow after charity, and desire spiritual gifts, but rather that ye may prophesy.

5. I would that ye all spake with tongues, but rather that ye prophesied; for greater is he that prophesieth than he that speaketh with tongues, except he interpret, that the church may receive edifying.

12. Even so ye, forasmuch as ye are zealous of spiritual gifts, seek that ye may excel to the edifying of the church.—1 *Cor.* 15.

6. Having then gifts differing according to the grace that is given to us, whether prophecy, let us prophesy according to the proportion of faith;

7. Or ministry, let us wait on our ministering: or he that teacheth, on teaching.—*Rom.* 12.

17. That the God of our Lord Jesus Christ, the Father of glory, may give unto you the spirit of wisdom and revelation in the knowledge of him.—*Eph.* 1.

DIVINE AUTHORITY

BY WHICH ALONE, MEN ARE EMPOWERED TO ACT IN THE NAME OF THE LORD OR OFFICIATE IN THE SACRED ORDINANCES OF THE GOSPEL.

Necessity of it:

14. How then shall they call on him in whom they have not believed? and how shall they believe in him of whom they have not heard? and how shall they hear without a preacher?

15. And how shall they preach, except they be sent? as it is written, How beautiful are the feet of them that preach the gospel of peace, and bring glad tidings of good things!—*Rom.* 10.

11. If any man speak, let him speak as the oracles of God; if any man minister, let him do it as of the ability which God giveth: that God in all things may be glorified through Jesus Christ, to whom be praise and dominion for ever and ever. Amen.—1 *Pet.* 4.

4. And no man taketh this honor unto himself, but he that is called of God, as was Aaron. —*Heb.* 5.

20. Now then we are ambassadors for Christ, as though God did beseech you by us: we pray you in Christ's stead, be ye reconciled to God. —2 *Cor.* 2.

Given to the Apostles:

16. Ye have not chosen me, but I have chosen you, and ordained you, that ye should go and bring forth fruit, and that your fruit should remain: that whatsoever ye shall ask of the Father in my name, he may give it you.— *John* 15.

14. And he ordained twelve, that they *Given to the Apostles:* should be with him, and that he might send them forth to preach,

15. And to have power to heal sicknesses, and to cast out devils.—*Mark* 3.

21. And said Jesus to them again, Peace be unto you: as my father hath sent me, even so send I you.

22. And when he had said this, he breathed on them, and said unto them, Receive ye the Holy Ghost:.

23. Whose soever sins ye remit, they are remitted unto them; and whose soever sins ye retain, they are retained.—*John* 20.

18. Verily I say unto you, Whatsoever ye shall bind on earth shall be bound in heaven: and whatsoever ye shall loose on earth shall be loosed in heaven.—*Matt.* 18

14. And the anger of the Lord was kindled *Called by Revelation:* against Moses, and he said, Is not Aaron the Levite thy brother? I know that he can speak well. And also, behold, he cometh forth to meet thee: and when he seeth thee, he will be glad in his heart.

15. And thou shalt speak unto him, and put words in his mouth: and I will be with thy mouth; and with his mouth, and will teach you what ye shall do.—*Ex.* 4.

1. And take thou unto thee Aaron thy brother, and his sons with him, from among the children of Israel, that he may minister unto me in the priest's office, even Aaron, Nadab and Abihu, Eleazer and Ithamar, Aaron's sons.—*Ex.* 28.

18. And the Lord said unto Moses, Take *How author- ity was conferred:* thee Joshua the son of Nun, a man in whom is the spirit, and lay thine hand upon him;— *Num.* 27.

*How author-
ity was
conferred:*
19. And set him before Eleazer the priest, and before all the congregation; and give him a charge in their sight.

20. And thou shalt put some of thine honor upon him, that all the congregation of the children of Israel may be obedient.

22. And Moses did as the Lord commanded him: and he took Joshua, and set him before Eleazer the priest, and before all the congregation:

23. And he laid his hands upon him, and gave him a charge, as the Lord commanded by the hand of Moses.—*Num.* 27.

9. And Joshua the son of Nun was full of the spirit of wisdom; for Moses had laid his hands upon him: and the children of Israel hearkened unto him, and did as the Lord commanded Moses.—*Deut.* 34.

5. And the saying pleased the whole multitude: and they chose Stephen, a man full of faith and of the Holy Ghost, and Philip, and Prochorus, and Nicanor, and Timon, and Parmenas, and Nicolas a proselyte of Antioch:

6. Whom they set before the apostles: and when they had prayed, they laid their hands on them.—*Acts* 6.

1. Now there were in the church that was at Antioch certain prophets and teachers; as Barnabas, and Simeon that was called Niger, and Lucius of Cyrene, and Manaen, which had been brought up with Herod the tetrarch, and Saul.

2. As they ministered to the Lord, and fasted, the Holy Ghost said, Separate me Barnabas and Saul for the work whereunto I have called them.

3. And when they had fasted and prayed, and laid their hands on them, they sent them away.—*Acts* 13.

APOSTASY FROM THE GOSPEL.

5. The earth also is defiled under the inhabitants thereof; because they have transgressed the laws, changed the ordinance, broken the everlasting covenant.

6. Therefore hath the curse devoured the earth, and they that dwell therein are desolate: therefore the inhabitants of the earth are burned, and few men left.—*Isa.* 24.

13. For my people have committed two evils; they have forsaken me the fountain of living waters, and hewed them out cisterns, broken cisterns, that can hold no water.—*Jer.* 2.

19. O Lord, my strength, and my fortress, and my refuge in the day of affliction, the Gentiles shall come unto thee from the ends of the earth, and shall say, Surely our fathers have inherited lies, vanity, and things wherein there is no profit.

20. Shall a man make gods unto himself, and they are no gods?

21. Therefore, behold, I will this once cause them to know, I will cause them to know mine hand and my might; and they shall know that my name is The Lord.—*Jer.* 16.

3. Let no man deceive you by any means: for that day shall not come, except there come a falling away first, and that man of sin be revealed, the son of perdition;

4. Who opposeth and exalteth himself above all that is called God, or that is worshiped; so that he as God sitteth in the temple of God, showing himself that he is God.—2 *Thes.* 2.

Foretold:

3. For the time will come when they will not endure sound doctrine; but after their own lusts shall they heap to themselves teachers, having itching ears;

4. And they shall turn away their ears from the truth, and shall be turned unto fables.—2 *Tim.* 4.

Universal:

1. Behold, the Lord maketh the earth empty, and maketh it waste, and turneth it upside down, and scattereth abroad the inhabitants thereof.

2. And it shall be, as with the people, so with the priest; as with the servant, so with his master; as with the maid, so with her mistress; as with the buyer, so with the seller; as with the lender, so with the borrower; as with the taker of usury, so with the giver of usury to him.

3. The land shall be utterly emptied, and utterly spoiled: for the Lord hath spoken this word.

5. The earth also is defiled under the inhabitants thereof; because they have transgressed the laws, changed the ordinance, broken the everlasting covenant.—*Isa.* 24.

11. Behold, the days come, saith the Lord God, that I will send a famine in the land, not a famine of bread, not a thirst for water, but of hearing the words of the Lord:

12. And they shall wander from sea to sea, and from the north even to the east, they shall run to and fro to seek the word of the Lord, and shall not find it.—*Amos.* 8.

4. And they worshiped the dragon which gave power unto the beast: and they worshiped the beast, saying, Who is like unto the beast? who is able to make war with him? —*Rev.* 13.

5. And there was given unto him a mouth *Universal:* speaking great things and blasphemies; and power was given unto him to continue forty and two months.

6. And he opened his mouth in blasphemy against God, to blaspheme his name, and his tabernacle, and them that dwell in heaven.

7. And it was given unto him to make war with the saints, and to overcome them: and power was given him over all kindreds, and tongues, and nations.

8. And all that dwell upon the earth shall worship him, whose names are not written in the book of life of the Lamb slain from the foundation of the world.—*Rev.* 13.

10. And then shall many be offended, and *Internal* shall betray one another, and shall hate one *causes:* another.

11. And many false prophets shall rise, and shall deceive many.

12. And because iniquity shall abound, the love of many shall wax cold.

13. But he that shall endure unto the end, the same shall be saved.—*Matt.* 24.

29. For I know this, that after my departing shall grievous wolves enter in among you, not sparing the flock.

30. Also of your own selves shall men arise speaking perverse things, to draw away disciples after them.—*Acts* 20.

1. Now the Spirit speaketh expressly, that in the latter times some shall depart from the faith, giving heed to seducing spirits, and doctrines of devils;

2. Speaking lies in hypocrisy; having their conscience seared with a hot iron.—1 *Tim.* 4.

Internal causes: 3. Forbidding to marry, and commanding to abstain from meats, which God hath created to be received with thanksgiving of them which believe and know the truth.—1 *Tim.* 4.

1. But there were false prophets also among the people, even as there shall be false teachers among you who privily shall bring in damnable heresies, even denying the Lord that bought them, and bring upon themselves swift destruction.

2. And many shall follow their pernicious ways; by reason of whom the way of truth shall be evil spoken of.

3. And through covetousness shall they with feigned words make merchandise of you: whose judgment now of a long time lingereth not, and their damnation slumbereth not —2 *Pet.* 2.

17. But, beloved, remember ye the words which were spoken before of the apostles of our Lord Jesus Christ;

18. How that they told you there should be mockers in the last time, who should walk after their own ungodly lusts. —*Jude.*

Already commenced in Paul's time: 6. I marvel that ye are so soon removed from him that called you into the grace of Christ unto another gospel:

7. Which is not another; but there be some that trouble you, and would pervert the gospel of Christ.—*Gal.* 1.

7. For the mystery of iniquity doth already work: only he who now letteth will let, until he be taken out of the way.

8. And then shall that Wicked be revealed, whom the Lord shall consume with the spirit of his mouth, and shall destroy with the brightness of his coming:—2 *Thes.* 2.

9. Even him, whose coming is after the *Already com-*
working of Satan with all power and signs and *menced in*
lying wonders. *Paul's time:*

11. And for this cause God shall send them
strong delusion, that they should believe a lie:

12. That they all might be damned who
believed not the truth, but had pleasure in
unrighteousness.—2 *Thes.* 2.

4. For there are men crept in unawares, who
were before of old ordained to this condemnation, ungodly men, turning the grace of our
God into lasciviousness, and denying the only
Lord God, and our Lord Jesus Christ.—*Jude.*

21. I beheld, and the same horn made war *External*
with the Saints, and prevailed against them; *causes:*

22. Until the Ancient of Days came, and
judgment was given to the saints of the Most
High; and the time came that the saints possessed the kingdom.

23. Thus he said, The fourth beast shall be
the fourth kingdom upon the earth, which shall
be diverse from all kingdoms, and shall devour
the whole earth, and shall tread it down, and
break it to pieces.

24. And the ten horns out of his kingdom
are ten kings that shall arise: and another shall
rise after them; and he shall be diverse from
the first, and he shall subdue three kings.

25. And he shall speak great words against
the Most High, and shall wear out the Saints of
the Most High, and think to change times and
laws: and they shall be given into his hand
until a time and times and the dividing of
time.—*Dan.* 7:

9. Then shall they deliver you up to be
afflicted, and shall kill you: and ye shall be
hated of all nations for my name's sake.—
Matt. 24.

External causes: 2. They shall put you out of the synagogues: yea, the time cometh, that whosoever killeth you will think that he doeth God service.

3. And these things will they do unto you, because they have not known the Father, nor me.—*John* 16.

7. And it was given unto him to make war with the saints, and to overcome them: and power was given him over all kindreds, and tongues, and nations.

8. And all that dwell upon the earth shall worship him, whose names are not written in the book of life of the Lamb slain from the foundation of the world.—*Rev.* 13.

Present condition of the world predicted: 9. Stay yourselves, and wonder; cry ye out, and cry: they are drunken, but not with wine; they stagger, but not with strong drink.

10. For the Lord hath poured out upon you the spirit of deep sleep, and hath closed your eyes: the prophets and your rulers, the seers hath he covered.

13. Wherefore the Lord said, Forasmuch as this people draw near me with their mouth, and with their lips do honor me, but have removed their heart far from me, and their fear toward me is taught by the precept of men:

14. Therefore, behold, I will proceed to do a marvelous work among this people, even a marvelous work and a wonder: for the wisdom of their wise men shall perish, and the understanding of their prudent men shall be hid.—*Isa.* 29.

7. But they also have erred through wine, and through strong drink are out of the way; the priest and the prophet have erred through strong drink, they are swallowed up of wine, they are out of the way through strong drink; they err in vision, they stumble in judgment. —*Isa.* 28.

2. For, behold, the darkness shall cover the earth, and gross darkness the people: but the Lord shall arise upon thee, and his glory shall be seen upon thee.—*Isa.* 60. *Present condition of the world predicted*

5. Thus saith the Lord concerning the prophets that make my people err, that bite with their teeth, and cry, Peace; and he that putteth not into their mouths, they even prepare war against him.

6. Therefore night shall be unto you, that ye shall not have a vision; and it shall be dark unto you, that ye shall not divine; and the sun shall go down over the prophets, and the day shall be dark over them.

7. Then shall the seers be ashamed, and the diviners confounded: yea, they shall all cover their lips; for there is no answer of God.

11. The heads thereof judge for reward, and the priests thereof teach for hire, and the prophets thereof divine for money: yet will they lean upon the Lord, and say, Is not the Lord among us? none evil can come upon us. —*Mic.* 3.

10. For the land is full of adulterers; for because of swearing the land mourneth; the pleasant places of the wilderness are dried up, and their course is evil, and their force is not right.

11. For both prophet and priest are profane; yea, in my house have I found their wickedness, saith the Lord.

12. Wherefore their way shall be unto them as slippery ways in the darkness: they shall be driven on, and fall therein: for I will bring evil upon them, even the year of their visitation, saith the Lord.—*Jer.* 23.

*Present con-
dition of the
world fore-
told:* 1. Hear the word of the Lord, ye children of Israel: for the Lord hath a controversy with the inhabitants of the land, because there is no truth, no mercy, nor knowledge of God, in the land.

2. By swearing, and lying, and killing, and stealing, and committing adultery, they break out, and blood toucheth blood.

6. My people are destroyed for lack of knowl-edge: because thou hast rejected knowledge, I will also reject thee, that thou shalt be no priest to me: seeing thou hast forgotten the law of thy God, I will also forget thy children.

7. As they were increased, so they sinned against me: therefore I will change their glory into shame.

8. They eat up the sin of my people, and they set their heart on their iniquity.

9. And there shall be, like people, like priest: and I will punish them for their ways, and reward them for their doings.

10. For they shall eat and not have enough: they shall commit whoredom and shall not increase: because they have left off to take heed to the Lord.— *Hos.* 4.

13. For my people have committed two evils; they have forsaken me, the fountain of living waters, and hewed them out cisterns, broken cisterns, that can hold no water.—*Jer.* 2.

31. The prophets prophesy falsely, and the priests bear rule by their means; and my people love to have it so: and what will ye do in the end thereof?—*Jer.* 5.

8. This people draweth nigh unto me with their mouth, and honoreth me with their lips; but their heart is far from me.

9. But in vain do they worship me, teachin for doctrines the commandments of men.— *Matt.* 15.

11. And for this cause God shall send them *Present con-* strong delusion, that they should believe a lie: *dition of the world fore-*

12. That they all might be damned who *told:* believed not the truth, but had pleasure in unrighteousness.—2 *Thes.* 2.

1. This know also, that in the last days perilous times shall come.

2. For men shall be lovers of their own selves, covetous, boasters, proud, blasphemers, disobedient to parents, unthankful, unholy,

3. Without natural affection, trucebreakers, false accusers, incontinent, fierce, despisers of those that are good,

4. Traitors, heady, highminded, lovers of pleasures more than lovers of God;

5. Having a form of godliness, but denying the power thereof: from such turn away.

6. For of this sort are they which creep into houses, and lead captive silly women laden with sins, led away with divers lusts,

7. Ever learning and never able to come to the knowledge of the truth.

8. Now as Jannes and Jambres withstood Moses, so do these also resist the truth: men of corrupt minds, reprobate concerning the faith.

9. But they shall proceed no further: for their folly shall be manifest unto all men, as theirs also was.—2 *Tim.* 3.

3. For the time will come when they will not endure sound doctrine; but after their own lusts shall they heap to themselves teachers, having itching ears;

4. And they shall turn away their ears from the truth, and shall be turned unto fables.—2 *Tim.* 4.

Present con-
dition of the
world fore-
told.
3. Knowing this first, that there shall come
in the last days scoffers; walking after their
own lusts,

4. And saying, Where is the promise of his
coming? for since the fathers fell asleep, all
things continue as they were from the beginning of the creation.—2 *Pet.* 3.

17. But, beloved, remember ye· the words
which were spoken before of the apostles of our
Lord Jesus Christ;

18. How that they told you there should be
mockers in the last time, who should walk after
their own ungodly lusts.—*Jude.*

19. O Lord, my strength and my fortress,
and my refuge in the day of affliction, the
Gentiles shall come unto thee from the ends of
the earth, and shall say, Surely our fathers
have inherited lies, vanity, and things wherein
there is no profit.—*Jer.* 16.

NOTE.—Not only is the apostasy from primitive Christianity
amply proven by the present condition of the world—the absence
of such officers in the various churches as the Savior instituted,
the changes in the ordinances, etc.—but it is not difficult to trace
in the writings of historians and commentators of repute how
and when various changes took place.

Mosheim, in his "Ecclesiastical History," says of the second
century, A.D.:

"The Christian bishops multiplied sacred rites for the sake
of rendering the Jews and pagans more friendly to them."

"A large part, therefore, of the Christian observances and
institutions, even in this century, had the aspect of pagan
mysteries."

"The noble simplicity and majestic dignity of the Christian
religion were lost or at least impaired, when these philosphers
presumed to associate their dogmas wit ι it, and to bring faith
and piety under the dominion of human reason."

Of the third century he says: "All the monuments of this
century which have come down to us show that there was a great
increase of ceremonies. * * * Baptism was publicly administered twice a year to candidates who had gone through a long
preparation and trial. * * * None were admitted to the sacred
font until the exorcist, by a solemn and menacing formula,
had declared them free from bondage to the prince of darkness
and now servants of God."

Of the fourth century he writes: "The Christian bishops introduced with but slight alterations into the Christian worship, those rites or institutions by which formerly the Greeks and Romans and other nations had manifested their reverence towards their imaginary deities."

In the fifth century it is said: "The superstitious notions and human devices by which religion was before much clogged, were very considerably augmented. The aid of departed Saints was implored with supplications by vast multitudes, and no one censured this absurd devotion." * * * "The whole Christian church was in this century overwhelmed with these disgraceful fictions."

Of the sixth century he says: "The barriers of the primitive simplicity and truth being once violated, the state of theology waxed worse; and the amount of the impure and superstitious additions to the religion of Christ is almost indescribable."

"During this [the seventh] century true religion lay buried under a senseless mass of superstitions, and was unable to raise her head. The earlier Christians had worshiped only God and His Son, but those called Christians in this century worshiped the wood of a cross, the images of holy men, and bones of dubious origin."

And so through later centuries may departures from the true faith and evidences of a complete apostasy be traced. And some of the most intelligent and honest religionists of the past few centuries have not only discovered but been frank enough to acknowledge the apostate condition of Christendom.

Mr. Wesley states that the reason the gifts are no longer in the church, "is because the love of many waxed cold, and the Christians had turned heathen again, and had only a dead form left." (See Vol. I, Sermon 94.)

Smith's Bible Dictionary (page 163) also says: "We must not expect to see the church of holy scriptures actually existing in its perfection on the earth. It is not to be found thus perfect either in the collected fragments of Christendom, or still less in any one of those fragments."

Dr. Adam Clark, in his commentaries (page 452) on the 4th chapter of Ephesians, says: "All these officers and the gifts and graces conferred upon them were judged necessary by the Great Head of the church, for its full instruction in the important doctrines of Christianity. The same *officers* and *gifts* are still necessary, and God gives them, but they *do not know their places.*"

Roger Williams refused to continue as pastor over the oldest Baptist church in America on the grounds that there was "no regularly constituted church on earth, nor any person authorized to administer any church ordinance: nor can there be, until new apostles are sent by the Great Head of the church for whose coming I am seeking." (See "Picturesque America," page 502.)

"Till that great and notable day of the Lord come, we cannot, from the prophetic word, anticipate a universal RETURN, *to the original gospel,* or a general restoration of the kingdom of God in its primitive form." ("Christianity Restored." Alex. Campbell. Page 181.)

RESTORATION OF THE GOSPEL,

AND THE ESTABLISHMENT OF THE KINGDOM OF GOD.

To be restored: 44. And in the days of these kings shall the God of heaven set up a kingdom, which shall never be destroyed: and the kingdom shall not be left to other people, but it shall break in pieces and consume all these kingdoms, and it shall stand forever.

45. Forasmuch as thou sawest that the stone was cut out of the mountain without hands, and that it brake in pieces the iron, the brass, the clay, the silver, and the gold; the great God hath made known to the king what shall come to pass hereafter: and the dream is certain, and the interpretation thereof sure.—*Dan. 2.*

How restored: 6. And I saw another angel fly in the midst of heaven, having the everlasting gospel to preach unto them that dwell on the earth, and to every nation, and kindred, and tongue, and people,

7. Saying with a loud voice, Fear God, and give glory to him; for the hour of his judgment is come: and worship him that made heaven, and earth, and the sea, and the fountains of waters.—*Rev. 14.*

To whom: 1. I lifted up mine eyes again, and looked, and behold a man with a measuring line in his hand.

2. Then said I, Whither goest thou? And he said unto me, to measure Jerusalem, to see what is the breadth thereof, and what is the length thereof.

3. And, behold, the angel that talked with me went forth, and another angel went out to meet him,—*Zech. 2.*

4. And said unto him, Run, speak to this *To whom:*
young man, saying, Jerusalem shall be inhabited
as towns without walls for the multitude of
men and cattle therein:

5. For I, saith the Lord, will be unto her a
wall of fire round about, and will be the glory
in the midst of her.—*Zech.* 2.

28. But there is a God in heaven that re- *When to be*
vealeth secrets, and maketh known to the *restored:*
king Nebuchadnezzar what shall be in the
latter days. Thy dream, and the visions of
thy head upon thy bed, are these;

29. As for thee, O king, thy thoughts came
into thy mind upon thy bed, what should
come to pass hereafter: and he that revealeth
secrets maketh known to thee what shall come
to pass.

44. And in the days of these kings shall
the God of heaven set up ·a kingdom, which
shall never be destroyed: and the kingdom
shall not be left to other people, but it shall
break in pieces and consume all these kingdoms, and it shall stand forever.

45. Forasmuch as thou sawest that the stone
was cut out of the mountain without hands,
and that it brake in pieces the iron, the brass,
the clay, the silver, and the gold; the great
God hath made known to the king what shall
come to pass hereafter: and the dream is certain, and the interpretation thereof sure.—
Dan. 2.

27. And the kingdom and dominion, and
the greatness of the kingdom under the whole
heaven, shall be given to the people of the
saints of the Most High, whose kingdom is an
everlasting kingdom, and all dominions shall
serve and obey him.—*Dan.* 7.

When to be restored: 14. And this gospel of the kingdom shall be preached in all the world for a witness unto all nations; and then shall the end come.—*Mat.* 24.

7. Saying with a loud voice, Fear God, and give glory to him; for the hour of his judgment is come: and worship him that made heaven, and earth, and the sea, and the fountains of waters.

8. And there followed another angel, saying, Babylon is fallen, is fallen, that great city, because she made all nations drink of the wine of the wrath of her fornication.—*Rev.* 14.

25. For I would not, brethren, that ye should be ignorant of this mystery, (lest ye should be wise in your own conceits) that blindness in part is happened to Israel, until the fulness of the Gentiles be come in.

26. And so all Israel shall be saved: as it is written, There shall come out of Sion the Deliverer, and shall turn away ungodliness from Jacob.—*Rom.* 11.

19. Repent ye therefore, and be converted, that your sins may be blotted out, when the times of refreshing shall come from the presence of the Lord;

20. And he shall send Jesus Christ, which before was preached unto you:

21. Whom the heaven must recieve, until the times of restitution of all things, which God hath spoken by the mouth of all his holy prophets, since the world began.—*Acts.* 3.

9. They shall not hurt nor destroy in all my holy mountain: for the earth shall be full of the knowledge of the Lord, as the waters cover the sea.—*Isa.* 11.

THE SCATTERING OF ISRAEL.

33. And I will scatter you among the heathen, *Predictions*
and will draw out a sword after you: and *concerning*
your land shall be desolate, and your cities *it:*
waste.—*Lev.* 26.

27. And the Lord shall scatter you among
the nations, and ye shall be left few in number
among the heathen, whither the Lord shall
lead you.—*Deut.* 4.

63. And it shall come to pass, that as the
Lord rejoiced over you to do you good, and to
multiply you; so the Lord will rejoice over
you to destroy you, and to bring you to
naught; and ye shall be plucked from off the
land whither thou goest to possess it.

64. And the Lord shall scatter thee among
all people, from the one end of the earth even
unto the other; and there thou shalt serve
other gods, which neither thou nor thy
fathers have known, even wood and stone.—
Deut. 28.

14. Thus saith the Lord against all mine evil
neighbors, that touch the inheritance which I
have caused my people Israel to inherit; Behold,
I will pluck them out of their land, and pluck
out the house of Judah from among them.

15. And it shall come to pass, after that I
have plucked them out I will return, and have
compassion on them, and will bring them again,
every man to his heritage, and every man to
his land.—*Jer.* 12.

9. For, lo, I will command, and I will sift
the house of Israel among all nations, like as
corn is sifted in a sieve, yet shall not the least
grain fall upon the earth.—*Amos* 9.

*Predictions
concerning
it:*

24. And they shall fall by the edge of the sword, and shall be led away captive into all nations: and Jerusalem shall be trodden down of the Gentiles, until the times of the Gentiles be fulfilled.—*Luke* 21.

16. Know that thus saith the Lord of the king that sitteth upon the throne of David, and of all the people that dwelleth in this city, and of your brethren that are not gone forth with you into captivity;

17. Thus saith the Lord of hosts; Behold, I will send upon them the sword, the famine, and the pestilence, and will make them like vile figs, that cannot be eaten, they are so evil.

18. And I will persecute them with the sword, with the famine, and with the pestilence, and will deliver them to be removed to all the kingdoms of the earth, to be a curse, and an astonishment, and an hissing, and a reproach, among all the nations whither I have driven them:

*Reason for
the
scattering:*

19. Because they have not harkened to my words, saith the Lord, which I sent unto them by my servants and prophets, rising up early and sending them; but ye would not hear, saith the Lord.—*Jer.* 29.

23. And I lifted up mine hand unto them also in the wilderness, that I would scatter them among the heathen, and disperse them through the countries;

24. Because they had not executed my judgments, but had despised my statutes, and had polluted my sabbaths, and their eyes were after their fathers' idols.—*Ezek.* 20.

14. But I scattered them with a whirlwind among all the nations whom they knew not. Thus the land was desolate after them, that no man passed through nor returned: for they laid the pleasant land desolate.—*Zech.* 7.

GATHERING OF ISRAEL.

1. And it shall come to pass, when all these *Israel to be* things are upon thee, the blessing and the *gathered:* curse, which I have set before thee, and thou shalt call them to mind among all the nations, whither the Lord thy God hath driven thee,

2. And shalt return unto the Lord thy God, and shalt obey his voice according to all that I command thee this day, thou and thy children, with all thine heart, and with all thy soul;

3. That then the Lord thy God will turn thy captivity, and have compassion upon thee, and will return and gather thee from all the nations, whither the Lord thy God hath scattered thee.

4. If any of thine be driven out unto the outmost parts of heaven, from thence will the Lord thy God gather thee, and from thence will he fetch thee;

5. And the Lord thy God will bring thee into the land which thy father possessed, and thou shalt possess it; and he will do thee good, and multiply thee above thy fathers.— *Deut.* 30.

8. Remember, I beseech thee, the word that thou commandest thy servant Moses, saying, If ye transgress, I will scatter you abroad among the nations:

9. But if ye turn unto me, and keep my commandments, and do them; though there were of you cast out unto the uttermost part of the heaven, yet will I gather them from thence, and will bring them unto the place that I have chosen to set my name there.—*Neh.* 1.

*Israel to be
gathered:*   14. Turn, O backsliding children, saith the
Lord; for I am married unto you: and I will
take you one of a city, and two of a family,
and I will bring you to Zion:

15. And I will give you pastors according to
mine heart, which shall feed you with knowledge and understanding.—*Jer.* 3.

14. Thus saith the Lord against all mine evil
neighbors, that touch the inheritance which I
have caused my people Israel to inherit; Behold,
I will pluck them out of their land, and pluck
out the house of Judah from among them.

15. And it shall come to pass, after that I
have plucked them out I will return, and have
compassion on them, and will bring them again,
every man to his heritage, and every man to
his land.—*Jer.* 12.

3. And I will gather the remnant of my
flock out of all countries whither I have driven
them, and will bring them again to their folds;
and they shall be fruitful and increase.

4. And I will set up shepherds over them
which shall feed them: and they shall fear no
more, nor be dismayed, neither shall they be
lacking, saith the Lord.—*Jer.* 23.

10. Hear the word of the Lord, O ye nations,
and declare it in the isles afar off, and say, He
that scattered Israel will gather him, and keep
him, as a shepherd doth his flock.

11. For the Lord hath redeemed Jacob, and
ransomed him from the hand of him that was
stronger than he.

12. Therefore they shall come and sing in
the height of Zion, and shall flow together to
the goodness of the Lord, for wheat and for
wine, and for oil, and for the young of the
flock and of the herd: and their soul shall be
as a watered garden; and they shall not sorrow any more at all.—*Jer.* 31.

37. Behold, I will gather them out of all *Israel to be* countries whither I have driven them in mine *gathered:* anger, and in my fury, and in great wrath; and I will bring them again unto this place, and I will cause them to dwell safely:

38. And they shall be my people, and I will be their God:

39. And I will give them one heart, and one way, that they may fear me for ever, for the good of them, and of their children after them. —*Jer.* 32.

7. And I will cause the captivity of Judah and the captivity of Israel to return, and will build them, as at the first.

8. And I will cleanse them from all their iniquity, whereby they have sinned against me; and I will pardon all their iniquities, whereby they have sinned, and whereby they have transgressed against me.

9. And it shall be to me a name of joy, a praise and an honor before all the nations of the earth, which shall hear all the good that I do unto them: and they shall fear and tremble for all the goodness and for all the prosperity that I procure unto it.

10. Thus saith the Lord; Again there shall be heard in this place, which ye say shall be desolate without man and without beast, even in the cities of Judah, and in the streets of Jerusalem, that are desolate, without man, and without inhabitant, and without beast,

11. The voice of joy, and the voice of glad-ness, the voice of the bridegroom, and the voice of the bride, the voice of them that shall say, Praise the Lord of hosts: for the Lord is good; for his mercy endureth for ever: and of them that shall bring the sacrifice of praise into the

Israel to be gathered: house of the Lord   For I will cause to return the captivity of the land, as at first, saith the Lord.—*Jer.* 33.

4. In those days, and in that time, saith the Lord, the children of Israel shall come, they and the children of Judah together, going and weeping: they shall go, and seek the Lord their God.

5. They shall ask the way to Zion with their faces thitherward, saying, Come, and let us join ourselves to the Lord in a perpetual covenant that shall not be forgotten.—*Jer.* 50.

To the top of the mountains: 1. But in the last days it shall come to pass, that the mountain of the house of the Lord shall be established in the top of the mountains, and it shall be exalted above the hills; and people shall flow unto it.

2. And many nations. shall come, and say, Come, and let us go up to the mountain of the Lord, and to the house of the God of Jacob; and he will teach us of his ways, and we will walk in his paths: for the law shall go forth of Zion, and the word of the Lord from Jerusalem. —*Mic.* 4.

Where from, Circumstances under which, etc. 1. O give thanks unto the Lord, for he is good: for his mercy endureth for ever.

2. Let the redeemed of the Lord say so, whom he hath redeemed from the hand of the enemy;

3. And gathered them out of the lands, from the east, and from the west, from the north and from the south.

4. They wandered in the wilderness in a solitary way; they found no city to dwell in. Hungry and thirsty, their soul fainted in them.—*Psal.* 107.

6. Then they cried unto the Lord in their *Where from,* trouble, and he delivered them out of their *Circum-stances under which,* distresses. *etc.*

7. And he led them forth by the right way, that they might go to a city of habitation.— *Psal.* 107.

26 And he will lift up an ensign to the nations from far, and will hiss unto them from the end of the earth: and, behold, they shall come with speed swiftly.—*Isa.* 5.

11. And it shall come to pass in that day, that the Lord shall set his hand again the second time to recover the remnant of his people, which shall be left, from Assyria, and from Egypt, and from Pathros, and from Cush, and from Elam, and from Shinar, and from Hamath, and from the islands of the sea.

12. And he will set up an ensign for the nations, and shall assemble the outcasts of Israel, and gather together the dispersed of Judah from the four corners of the earth.— *Isa.* 11.

4. Say to them that are of a fearful heart, Be strong, fear not: behold, your God will come with vengeance, even God with a recompence; he will come and save you.

5. Then the eyes of the blind shall be opened, and the ears of the deaf shall be unstopped.

6. Then shall the lame man leap as an hart, and the tongue of the dumb sing: for in the wilderness shall waters break out, and streams in the desert.

7. And the parched ground shall become a pool, and the thirsty land springs of water: in the habitation of dragons, where each lay, shall be grass with reeds and rushes.—*Isa.* 35.

Wherefrom,
Circum-
stances un-
der which,
etc.:

8. And an highway shall be there, and a way, and it shall be called The way of holiness; the unclean shall not pass over it; but it shall be for those: the wayfaring men, though fools, shall not err therein.

9. No lion shall be there, nor any ravenous beast shall go up thereon, it shall not be found there; but the redeemed shall walk there:

10. And the ransomed of the Lord shall return, and come to Zion with songs and everlasting joy upon their heads: they shall obtain joy and gladness, and sorrow and sighing shall flee away.—*Isa.* 35.

5. Fear not: for I am with thee: I will bring thy seed from the east, and gather thee from the west;

6. I will say to the north, Give up; and to the south, Keep not back: bring my sons from far, and my daughters from the ends of the earth;

7. Even every one that is called by my name: for I have created him for my glory, I have formed him; yea, I have made him.—*Isa.* 43.

11. Depart ye, depart ye, go ye out from thence, touch no unclean thing; go ye out of the midst of her; be ye clean, that bear the vessels of the Lord.

12. For ye shall not go out with haste, nor go by flight: for the Lord will go before you; and the God of Israel will be your rearward.—*Isa.* 52.

7. For a small moment have I forsaken thee; but with great mercies will I gather thee.—*Isa.*54.

18. In those days the house of Judah shall *Where from,* walk with the house of Israel, and they shall *Circum-* come together out of the land of the north to *stances un-* the land that I have given for an inheritance *der which,* unto your fathers. *etc.:*

19. But I said, How shall I put thee among the children, and give thee a pleasant land, a goodly heritage of the hosts of nations? and I said, Thou shalt call me, My father; and shalt not turn away from me.—*Jer.* 3.

14. Therefore, behold, the days come, saith the Lord, that it shall no more be said, The Lord liveth, that brought up the children of Israel out of the land of Egypt;

15. But, the Lord liveth, that brought up the children of Israel from the land of the north, and from all the lands whither he had driven them: and I will bring them again into their land that I gave unto their fathers.

16. Behold, I will send for many fishers, saith the Lord, and they shall fish them; and after will I send for many hunters, and they shall hunt them from every mountain, and from every hill, and out of the holes of the rocks.—*Jer.* 16.

8. Behold, I will bring them from the north country, and gather them from the coasts of the earth, and with them the blind and the lame, the woman with child and her that travaileth with child together: a great company shall return thither.

9. They shall come with weeping, and with supplications will I lead them: I will cause them to walk by the rivers of waters in a straight way, wherein they shall not stumble: for I am a father to Israel, and Ephraim is my firstborn.—*Jer.* 31.

Wherefrom, 34. And I will bring you out from the
Circum- people, and will gather you out of the countries
stances un- wherein ye are scattered, with a mighty hand,
der which, and with a stretched out arm, and with fury
etc.: poured out.

35. And I will bring you into the wilderness
of the people, and there will I plead with you
face to face.

36. Like as I' pleaded with your fathers in
the wilderness of the land of Egypt, so will I
plead with you, saith the Lord God.—*Ezek.*20.

9. I will not execute the fierceness of mine
anger, I will not return to destroy Ephraim:
for I am God, and not man; the Holy One in
the midst of thee: and I will not enter into the
city.

10. They shall walk after the Lord: he shall
roar like a lion: when he shall roar, then the
children shall tremble from the west.—*Hos.* 11.

31. And he shall send his angels with a great
sound of a trumpet, and they shall gather
together his elect from the four winds, from
one end of heaven to the other.—*Matt.* 24.

4. And I heard another voice from heaven,
saying, Come out of her, my people, that ye be
not partakers of her sins, and that ye receive
not of her plagues.—*Rev.* 18.

Promised 14. And the Lord said unto Abram, after·
inheritance : that Lot was separated from him, Lift up now
thine eyes, and look from the place where thou
art northward, and southward, and eastward,
and westward:

15. For all the land which thou seest, to
thee will I give it, and to thy seed forever.

16. And· I will make thy seed as the dust of
the earth: so that if a man can number the
dust of the earth, then shall thy seed also be
numbered.—*Gen.* 13.

17. Arise, walk through the land in the length of it and in the breadth of it; for I will give it unto thee.—*Gen.* 13.

Promised inheritance:

1. And there was a famine in the land, beside the first famine that was in the days of Abraham. And Isaac went unto Abimelech king of the Philistines unto Garar.

2. And the Lord appeared unto him, and said, Go not down into Egypt; dwell in the land which I shall tell thee of:

3. Sojourn in this land, and I will be with thee, and will bless thee; for unto thee, and unto thy seed, I will give all of these countries, and I will perform the oath which I sware unto Abraham thy father;

4. And I will make thy seed to multiply as the stars of heaven, and will give unto thy seed all these countries; and in thy seed shall all the nations of the earth be blessed.—*Gen.* 26.

3. And Jacob said unto Joseph, God Almighty appeared unto me at Luz in the land of Canaan, and blessed me,

4. And said unto me, behold, I will make thee fruitful, and multiply thee, and I will make of thee a multitude of people; and will give this land to thy seed after thee for an everlasting possession.

17. And when Joseph saw that his father laid his right hand upon the head of Ephraim, it displeased him: and he held up his father's hand, to remove it from Ephraim's head unto Manasseh's head.

18. And Joseph said unto his father, Not so, my father: for this is the firstborn; put thy right hand upon his head.—*Gen.* 48.

Promised inheritance: 19. And his father refused, and said, I know it, my son, I know it: he also shall become a people, and he also shall be great: but truly his younger brother shall be greater than he, and his seed shall become a multitude of nations.

20. And he blessed them that day, saying In thee shall Israel bless, saying, God make thee as Ephraim and as Manasseh: and he set Ephraim before Manasseh.—*Gen.* 48.

22. Joseph is a fruitful bough, even a fruitful bough by a well; whose branches run over the wall:

26. The blessings of thy father have prevailed above the blessings of my progenitors unto the utmost bound of the everlasting hills: they shall be on the head of Joseph, and on the crown of the head of him that was separate from his brethren.—*Gen.* 49.

13. And of Joseph he said, Blessed of the Lord be his land, for the precious things of heaven, for the dew, and for the deep that coucheth beneath,

14. And for the precious fruits brought forth by the sun, and for the precious things put forth by the moon,

15. And for the chief things of the ancient mountains, and for the precious things of the lasting hills,

16. And for the precious things of the earth and fulness thereof, and for the good will of him that dwelt in the bush: let the blessing come upon the head of Joseph, and upon the top of the head of him that was separated from his brethren.

17. His glory is like the firstling of his bullock, and his horns are like the horns of unicorns: with them he shall push the people

together to the ends of the earth: and they *Promised*
are the ten thousands of Ephraim, and they *inheritance:*
are the thousands of Manasseh.—*Deut.* 33.

9. For evildoers shall be cut off: but those
that wait upon the Lord, they shall inherit the
earth.

10. For yet a little while, and the wicked
shall not be: yea, thou shalt diligently consider his place, and it shall not be.

11. But the meek shall inherit the earth;
and shall delight themselves in the abundance
of peace.

22. For such as be blessed of him shall inherit the earth; and they that be cursed of
him shall be cut off.

28. For the Lord loveth judgment, and for-
saketh not his saints; they are preserved forever: but the seed of the wicked shall be cut off.

29. The righteous shall inherit the land,
and dwell therein for ever.—*Psal.* 37.

1. For the Lord will have mercy on Jacob,
and will yet choose Israel, and set them in
their own land: and the strangers shall be
joined with them, and they shall cleave to the
house of Jacob.

2. And the people shall take them, and
bring them to their place: and the house of
Israel shall possess them in the land of the
Lord for servants and handmaids: and they
shall take them captives, whose captives they
were; and they shall rule over their oppressors.
—*Isa.* 14.

17. No weapon that is formed against thee
shall prosper; and every tongue that shall rise
against thee in judgment thou shalt condemn.
This is the heritage of the servants of the
Lord, and their righteousness is of me, saith
the Lord.— *Isa.* 54.

12. For the nation and kingdom that will not serve thee shall perish; yea, those nations shall be utterly wasted.

'14. The sons also of them that afflicted thee shall come bending unto thee; and all they that despised thee shall bow themselves down at the soles of thy feet: and they shall call thee, The city of the Lord, The Zion of the Holy One of Israel.—*Isa.* 60.

4. And they shall build the old wastes, they shall raise up the former desolations, and they shall repair the waste cities, the desolations of many generations.

5. And strangers shall stand and feed your flocks, and the sons of the alien shall be your plowmen and your vinedressers.

6. But ye shall be named the Priests of the Lord: men shall call you the Ministers of our God: ye shall eat the riches of the Gentiles, and in their glory shall ye boast yourselves.

7. For your shame ye shall have double; and for confusion they shall rejoice in their portion: therefore in their land they shall possess the double: everlasting joy shall be unto them.

8. For I the Lord love judgment, I hate robbery for burnt offering; and I will direct their work in truth, and I will make an everlasting covenant with them.

9. And their seed shall be known among the Gentiles, and their offspring among the people: all that see them shall acknowledge them, that they are the seed which the Lord hath blessed.—*Isa.* 61.

12. Therefore they shall come and sing in the height of Zion, and shall flow together to the goodness of the Lord, for wheat, and for wine, and for oil, and for the young of the

flock and of the herd: and their soul shall be *Promised* as a watered garden; and they shall not sorrow *inheritance :* any more at all.

13. Then shall the virgin rejoice in the dance, both young men and old together: for I will turn their mourning into joy, and will comfort them, and make them rejoice from their sorrow.

14. And I will satiate the soul of the priests with fatness, and my people shall be satisfied with my goodness, saith the Lord.—*Jer.* 31. ʼ

21. And say unto them, Thus saith the Lord God; Behold I will take the children of Israel ,from among the heathen, whither they be gone, and will gather them on every side, and bring them into their own land:

22. And I will make them one nation in the land upon the mountains of Israel; and one king shall be king over them all: and they shall be no more two nations, neither shall they be divided into two kingdoms any more at all:

24. And David my servant shall be king over them; and they shall all have one shepherd: they shall also walk in my judgments, and observe my statutes, and do them.

26. Moreover I will make a covenant of peace with them; and it shall be an everlasting covenant with them; and I will place them and multiply them, and will set my sanctuary . in the midst of them for evermore.

27. My tabernacle also shall be with them: yea, I will be their God, and they shall be my people.—*Ezek.* 37.

27. And the kingdom and dominion, and the greatness of the kingdom under the whole heaven, shall be given to the people of the saints of the Most High, whose kingdom is an everlasting kingdom, and all dominions shall serve and obey him.—*Dan.* 7.

13. Behold, the days come, saith the Lord,
that the plowman shall overtake the reaper,
and the treader of grapes him that soweth
seed; and the mountains shall drop sweet wine,
and all the hills shall melt.

14. And I will bring again the captivity of
my people Israel, and they shall build the
waste cities, and inhabit them; and they shall
plant vineyards, and drink the wine thereof;
they shall also make gardens, and eat the fruit
of them.

15. And I will plant them upon their land,
and they shall no more be pulled up out of
their land which I have given them, saith the
Lord thy God.—*Amos.* 9.

3. And he shall judge among many people,
and rebuke strong nations afar off; and they
shall beat their swords into plowshares, and
their spears into pruning hooks: nation shall
not lift up a sword against nation, neither shall
they learn war any more.

4. But they shall sit every man under his
vine and under his fig tree; and none shall
make them afraid: for the mouth of the Lord
of hosts hath spoken it.—*Mic.* 4.

29. And I appoint unto you a kingdom, as
my Father hath appointed unto me;

30. That ye may eat and drink at my table
in my kingdom, and sit on thrones judging the
twelve tribes of Israel.—*Luke.* 12.

9. And they sung a new song, saying, Thou
art worthy to take the book, and to open the
seals thereof: for thou wast slain, and hast
redeemed us to God by thy blood out of every
kindred, and tongue, and people, and nation;

10. And hast made us unto our God kings
and priests: and we shall reign on the earth.—
Rev. 5.

SECOND COMING OF CHRIST.

25. For I know that my redeemer liveth, *Predictions concerning it:* and that he shall stand at the latter day upon the earth;

26. And though after my skin worms destroy this body; yet in my flesh shall I see God:

27. Whom I shall see for myself, and mine eyes shall behold, and not another; though my reins be consumed within me.—*Job* 19.

2. Out of Zion, the perfection of beauty, God hath shined.

3. Our God shall come, and shall not keep silence: a fire shall devour before him, and it shall be very tempestuous round about him.

4. He shall call to the heavens from above, and to the earth, that he may judge his people. —*Psal.* 50.

4. Say to them that are of a fearful heart, Be strong, fear not : behold, your God will come with vengeance, even God with a recompense; he will come and save you.—*Isa.* 35.

9. O Zion, that bringest good tidings, get thee up into the high mountain; O Jerusalem, that bringest good tidings, lift up thy voice with strength; lift it up, be not afraid; say unto the cities of Judah, Behold your God !

10. Behold, the Lord God will come with strong hand, and his arm shall rule for him: behold, his reward is with him, and his work before him.—*Isa.* 40.

28. So Christ was once offered to bear the sins of many; and unto them that look for him shall he appear the second time without sin unto salvation.—*Heb.* 9.

Predictions concerning it:

10. And while they looked steadfastly toward heaven as he went up, behold, two men stood by them in white apparel;

11. Which also said, Ye men of Galilee, why stand ye gazing up into heaven? this same Jesus, which is taken up from you into heaven, shall so come in like manner as ye have seen him go into heaven.—*Acts* 1.

19. Repent ye therefore, and be converted, that your sins may be blotted out, when the times of refreshing shall come from the presence of the Lord;

20. And he shall send Jesus Christ, which before was preached unto you:

21. Whom the heaven must receive until the times of restitution of all things, which God hath spoken by the mouth of all his holy prophets since the world began.—*Acts* 3.

Signs to precede his second coming:

14. And this Gospel of the kingdom shall be preached in all the world for a witness unto all nations; and then shall the end come.—*Matt:* 24.

26. And as it was in the days of Noe, so shall it be also in the days of the Son of man.

27. They did eat, they drank, they married wives, they were given in marriage, until the day that Noe entered into the ark, and the flood came, and destroyed them all.

28. Likewise also as it was in the days of Lot; they did eat, they drank, they bought, they sold, they planted, they builded;

29. But the same day that Lot went out of Sodom it rained fire and brimstone from heaven, and destroyed them all.

30. Even thus shall it be in the day when the son of man is revealed.—*Luke* 17.

10. Then said he unto them, Nation shall rise against nation, and kingdom against kingdom:—*Luke* 21.

11. And great earthquakes shall be in divers *Signs to pre-cede his second coming:* places, and famines, and pestilences: and fearful sights and great signs shall there be from heaven.

12. But before all these, they shall lay their hands on you, and persecute you, delivering you up to the synagogues, and into prisons, being brought before kings and rulers for my name's sake.

16. And ye shall be betrayed both by parents, and brethren, and kinsfolks, and friends; and some of you shall they cause to be put to death.

17. And ye shall be hated of all men for my name's sake.

25. And there shall be signs in the sun, and in the moon, and in the stars; and upon the earth distress of nations, with perplexity; the sea and the waves roaring;

26. Men's hearts failing them for fear, and for looking after those things which are coming on the earth: for the powers of heaven shall be shaken.

27. And then shall they see the Son of man coming in a cloud with power and great glory. —*Luke* 21.

12. And I beheld when he had opened the sixth seal, and, lo, there was a great earthquake; and the sun became black as sackcloth of hair, and the moon became as blood;

13. And the stars of heaven fell unto the earth, even as a fig tree casteth her untimely figs, when she is shaken of a mighty wind.

14. And the heaven departed as a scroll when it is rolled together; and every mountain and island were moved out of their places.

15. And the kings of the earth, and the great men, and the rich men, and the chief

Signs to pre-cede his sec-ond coming: captains, and the mighty men, and every bond-man, and every free man, hid themselves in the dens and in the rocks of the mountains;

16. And said to the mountains and rocks, Fall on us, and hide us from the face of him that sitteth on the throne, and from the wrath of the Lamb:

17. For the great day of his wrath is come; and who shall be able to stand?—*Rev.* 6.

How he will come: 38. Whosoever therefore shall be ashamed of me and of my words in this adulterous and sinful generation; of him also shall the Son of man be ashamed, when he cometh in the glory of his Father with the holy angels.—*Mark* 8.

26. And then shall they see the Son of man coming in the clouds with great power and glory.—*Mark* 13.

16. For the Lord himself shall descend from heaven with a shout, with the voice of the archangel, and with the trump of God: and the dead in Christ shall rise first.—1 *Thes.* 4.

7. And to you who are troubled rest with us, when the Lord Jesus shall be revealed from heaven with his mighty angels.

8. In flaming fire taking vengeance on them that know not God, and that obey not the gospel of our Lord Jesus Christ.—2 *Thes.* 1.

14. And Enoch also, the seventh from Adam, prophesied of these, saying, Behold, the Lord cometh with ten thousands of his saints,

15. To execute judgment upon all, and to convince all that are ungodly among them of all their ungodly deeds which they have ungodly committed, and of all their hard speeches which ungodly sinners have spoken against him.—*Jude.*

20. And the Redeemer shall come to Zion, *How he*
and unto them that turn from transgression in *will come:*
Jacob, saith the Lord.—*Isa.* 59.

15. The sun and moon shall be darkened,
and the stars shall withdraw their shining.

16. The Lord also shall roar out of Zion,
and utter his voice from Jerusalem; and the
heavens and the earth shall shake: but the
Lord will be the hope of his people, and the
strength of the children of Israel.

17. So shall you know that I am the Lord
your God dwelling in Zion, my holy mountain:
then shall Jerusalem be holy, and there shall
no strangers pass through her any more.—
Joel 3.

3. Then shall the Lord go forth, and fight *Where he*
against those nations, as when he fought in the *will come to:*
day of battle.

4. And his feet shall stand in that day upon
the mount of Olives, which is before Jerusalem
on the east, and the mount of Olives shall
cleave in the midst thereof toward the east
and toward the west, and there shall be a very
great valley; and half of the mountain shall
remove toward the north, and half of it toward
the south.

5. And ye shall flee to the valley of the
mountains; for the valley of the mountains
shall reach unto Azal: yea, ye shall flee, like
as ye fled from before the earthquake in the
days of Uzziah king of Judah: and the Lord
my God shall come, and all the Saints with
thee.—*Zech.* 14.

1. Behold, I will send my messenger, and he
shall prepare the way before me: and the Lord,
whom ye seek, shall suddenly come to his
temple, even the messenger of the covenant,
whom ye delight in: behold, he shall come,
saith the Lord of hosts.—*Mal.* 3.

THE ATONEMENT.

Christ's offering fore-told:
5. But he was wounded for our transgressions, he was bruised for our iniquities: the chastisement of our peace was upon him; and with his stripes we are healed.

6. All we like sheep have gone astray; we have turned every one to his own way; and the Lord hath laid on him the iniquity of us all.

8. He was taken from prison and from judgment: and who shall declare his generation? for he was cut off out of the land of the living: for the transgression of my people was he stricken.

11. He shall see of the travail of his soul, and shall be satisfied: by his knowledge shall my righteous servant justify many; for he shall bear their iniquities.

12. Therefore will I divide him a portion with the great, and he shall divide the spoil with the strong; because he hath poured out his soul unto death: and he was numbered with the transgressors; and he bare the sins of many, and made intercession for the transgressors.—*Isa.* 53.

19. And he took bread, and gave thanks, and brake it, and gave unto them, saying, This is my body which is given for you: this do in remembrance of me.

20. Likewise also the cup after supper, saying, this cup is the new testament in my blood, which is shed for you.—*Luke* 22.

29. The next day John seeth Jesus coming unto him, and saith, behold the Lamb of God, which taketh away the sin of the world.—*John* 1.

11. I am the good shepherd: the good shepherd giveth his life for the sheep.—*John* 10. *Christ's offering foretold:*

18. Forasmuch as ye know that ye were not redeemed with corruptible things, as silver and gold, from your vain conversation received by tradition from your fathers; *Foreordained:*

19. But with the precious blood of Christ, as of a lamb without blemish and without spot:

20. Who verily was foreordained before the foundation of the world, but was manifest in these last times for you,

21. Who by him do believe in God, that raised him up from the dead, and gave him glory; that your faith and hope might be in God.—1 *Pet.* 1.

8. And all that dwell upon the earth shall worship him, whose names are not written in the book of life of the Lamb slain from the foundation of the world.—*Rev.* 13.

8. Be not thou therefore ashamed of the testimony of our Lord, nor of me his prisoner: but be thou partaker of the afflictions of the gospel according to the power of God;

9. Who hath saved us, and called us with an holy calling, not according to our works, but according to his own purpose and grace, which was given us in Christ Jesus before the world began;

10. But is now made manifest by the appearing of our Savior Jesus Christ, who hath abolished death, and hath brought life and immortality to light through the gospel.—2 *Tim.* 1.

21. For since by man came death, by man came also the resurrection of the dead. *Original sin atoned for:*

22. For as in Adam all die, even so in Christ shall all be made alive.—1 *Cor.* 15.

Original sin atoned for: 12. Wherefore, as by one man sin entered into the world, and death by sin; and so death passed upon all men, for that all have sinned:

18. Therefore as by the offence of one judgment came upon all men to condemnation; even so by the righteousness of one the free gift came upon all men unto justification of life.

19. For as by one man's disobedience many were made sinners, so by the obedience of one shall many be made righteous.—*Rom.* 5.

15. And for this cause he is the mediator of the new testament, that by means of death, for the redemption of the transgressions that were under the first testament, they which are called might receive the promise of eternal inheritance.

16. For where a testament is, there must also of necessity be the death of the testator.

17. For a testament is in force after men are dead: otherwise it is of no strength at all while the testator liveth.

22. And almost all things are by the law purged with blood; and without shedding of blood is no remission.—*Heb.* 9.

Comprehensive nature of the atonement: 5. For there is one God, and one mediator between God and men, the man Christ Jesus;

6. Who gave himself a ransom for all, to be testified in due time.—1 *Tim.* 2.

32. And I, if I be lifted up from the earth, will draw all men unto me.—*John* 12.

9. But we see Jesus who was made little lower than the angels for the suffering of death, crowned with glory and honor; that he by the grace of God should taste death for every man. —*Heb.* 2.

2. And he is the propitiation for our sins: and not for ours only, but also for the sins of the whole world.—1 *John* 2.

Comprehensive nature of the atonement:

9. And they sung a new song, saying, Thou art worthy to take the book, and to open the seals thereof: for thou wast slain, and hast redeemed us to God by thy blood out of every kindred, and tongue, and people, and nation.— *Rev.* 5.

6. If we say that we have fellowship with him, and walk in darkness, we lie, and do not the truth: ·

Application to personal sins conditional:

7. But if we walk in the light, as he is in the light, we have fellowship one with another and the blood of Jesus Christ his Son cleanseth us from all sin.—1 *John* 1.

14. And as Moses lifted up the serpent in the wilderness, even so must the Son of man be lifted up:

15. That whosoever believeth in him should not perish, but have eternal life.—*John* 3.

10. For therefore we both labor and suffer reproach, because we trust in the living God, who is the Savior of all men, especially of those that believe.—1 *Tim.* 4.

28. Take heed therefore unto yourselves, and to all the flock, over the which the Holy Ghost hath made you overseers, to feed the church of God, which he hath purchased with his own blood.—*Acts* 20. ·

24. Being justified freely by his grace through the redemption that is in Christ Jesus:

25. Whom God hath set forth to be a propitiation through faith in his blood, to declare his righteousness for the remission of sins that are past, through the forbearance of God.— *Rom.* 3.

8

THE RESURRECTION.

Testimonies in regard to it: 25. For I know that my Redeemer liveth, and that he shall stand at the latter day upon the earth:

26. And though after my skin worms destroy this body, yet in my flesh shall I see God:

27. Whom I shall see for myself, and mine eyes shall behold and not another; though my reins be consumed within me.—*Job* 19.

10. For thou wilt not leave my soul in hell; neither wilt thou suffer thine Holy One to see corruption.—*Psal.* 16.

19. The dead men shall live, together with my dead body shall they arise. Awake and sing, ye that dwell in dust: for thy dew is as the dew of herbs, and the earth shall cast out the dead.—*Isa.* 26.

14. I will ransom them from the power of the grave; I will redeem them from death: O death, I will be thy plagues; O grave, I will be thy destruction: repentance shall be hid from mine eyes.—*Hos.* 13.

23. Jesus saith unto her, Thy brother shall rise again.

24. Martha saith unto him, I know that he shall rise again in the resurrection at the last day.

25. Jesus said unto her, I am the resurrection, and the life: he that believeth in me, though he were dead, yet shall he live.—*John* 11.

22. Having therefore obtained help of God, I continue unto this day, witnessing both to small and great, saying none other things than those which the prophets and Moses did say should come:—*Acts* 26.

23. That Christ should suffer, and that he *Testimonies* should be the first that should rise from the *in regard* dead, and should show light unto the people, *to it:* and to the Gentiles.—*Acts* 26.

21. Who shall change our vile body, that it may be fashioned like unto his glorious body, according to the working whereby he is able even to subdue all things unto himself.—*Phil.* 3.

5. And the angel answered and said unto *Already* the women, Fear not ye: for I know that ye *taken place:* seek Jesus, which was crucified.
6. He is not here: for he is risen, as he said. Come, see the place where the Lord lay.—*Matt.* 28.

32. This Jesus hath God raised up, whereof we all are witnesses.—*Acts* 2.

37. But he, whom God raised again, saw no corruption.—*Acts* 13.

52. And the graves were opened; and many bodies of the saints which slept arose,
53. And came out of the graves after his resurrection, and went into the holy city, and appeared unto many. —*Matt.* 27.

35. Women received their dead raised to life again: and others were tortured, not accepting deliverance; that they might obtain a better resurrection.—*Heb.* 11.

18. I am he that liveth, and was dead; and, behold, I am alive for evermore, Amen; and have the keys of hell and of death.—*Rev.* 1.

11. Then he said unto me, Son of man, these *Ezekiel's* bones are the whole house of Israel: Behold, *Vision:* they say, Our bones are dried, and our hope is lost: we are cut off for our parts.—*Ezek.* 37.

Ezekiel's Vision: 12. Therefore prophesy and say unto them, Thus saith the Lord God: Behold, O my people, I will open your graves, and cause you to come up out of your graves, and bring you into the land of Israel.

13. And ye shall know that I am the Lord, when I have opened your graves, O my people, and brought you up out of your graves,

14. And shall put my spirit in you, and ye shall live, and I shall place you in your own land: then shall ye know that I the Lord have spoken it, and performed it, saith the Lord.— *Ezek.* 37.

Universal: 28. Marvel not at this; for the hour is coming, in the which all that are in the graves shall hear his voice,

29. And shall come forth; they that have done good, unto the resurrection of life; and they that have done evil, unto the resurrection of damnation.—*John* 11.

32. And I, if I be lifted up from the earth, will draw all men unto me.—*John* 12.

15. And have hope toward God, which they themselves also allow, that there shall be a resurrection of the dead, both of the just and unjust.—*Acts* 24.

22. For as in Adam all die, even so in Christ shall all be made alive.

Order of the resurrection: 23. But every man in his own order: Christ the first-fruits; afterwards they that are Christ's at his coming.—1 *Cor.* 15.

14. For if we believe that Jesus died and rose again, even so them also which sleep in Jesus will God bring with him.

16. For the Lord himself shall descend from heaven with a shout, with the voice of the archangel, and with the trump of God: and the dead in Christ shall rise first:—*Thes.* 4.

17. Then we which are alive and remain *Order of the* shall be caught up together with them in the *resurrection:* clouds, to meet the Lord in the air: and so shall we be ever with the Lord.— 1 *Thes.* 4.

31. He seeing this before spake of the resurrection of Christ, that his soul was not left in hell, neither his flesh did see corruption.

32. For David is not ascended into the heavens: but he saith himself, The Lord said unto my Lord, Sit thou on my right hand.— *Acts.* 2.

·5. But the rest of the dead lived not again *Different* until the thousand years were finished. This *resurrections.* is the first resurrection.

6. Blessed and holy is he that hath part in the first resurrection: on such the second death hath no power, but they shall be priests of God and . of Christ, and shall reign with him a thousand years.—*Rev.* 20.

40. There are also celestial bodies and bodies *Different de-* terrestrial: but the glory of the celestial is one, *grees of* and the glory of the terrestrial is another *glory:*

41. There is one glory of the sun, and another glory of the moon, and another glory of the stars: for one star differeth from another star in glory.

42. So also is the resurrection of the dead. It is sown in corruption; it is raised in incorruption:

43. It is sown in dishonor; it is raised in glory: it is sown in weakness; it is raised in power:

44. It is sown a natural body; it is raised a spiritual body. There is a natural body, and there is a spiritual body.—1 *Cor.* 15.

2. In my Father's house are many mansions: if it were not so, I would have told you. I go to prepare a place for you.—*John* 14.

Different de-
grees of
glory:

2. I knew a man in Christ above fourteen years ago, (whether in the body, I cannot tell; or whether out of the body, I cannot tell: God knoweth;) such an one caught up to the third heaven.—*2 Cor.* 12.

Judgment to
follow the
resurrection:

12. And I saw the dead, small and great, stand before God; and the books were opened: and another book was opened, which is the book of life: and the dead were judged out of those things which were written in the books, according to their works.

13. And the sea gave up the dead which were in it; and death and hell delivered up the dead which were in them: and they were judged, every man according to their works.

14. And death and hell were cast into the lake of fire. This is the second death.

15. And whosoever was not found written in the book of life was cast into the lake of fire. —*Rev.* 20.

2. And many of them that sleep in the dust of the earth shall awake, some to everlasting life, and some to shame and everlasting contempt.—*Dan.* 12.

7. But the Lord shall endure for ever: he hath prepared his throne for judgment.

8. And he shall judge the world in righteousness, he shall minister judgment to the people in uprightness.

9. The Lord also will be a refuge for the oppressed, a refuge in times of trouble.

17. The wicked shall be turned into hell, and all the nations that forget God.—*Psal.* 9.

17. I said in mine heart, God shall judge the righteous and the wicked: for there is a time there for every purpose and for every work.—*Eccl.* 3.

17. Judgment also will I lay to the line, and *Judgment to follow the resurrection:* righteousness to the plummet: and the hail shall sweep away the refuge of lies, and the waters shall overflow the hiding place.—*Isa.*28.

9. I beheld till the thrones were cast down, and the Ancient of days did sit, whose garment was white as snow, and the hair of his head like the pure wool: his throne was like the fiery flame, and his wheels as burning fire.

10. A fiery stream issued and came forth from before him: thousand thousands ministered unto ·him, and ten thousand times ten thousand stood before him : the judgment was set, and the books were opened.

11. I beheld then because of the voice of the great words which the. horn spake: I beheld even till the beast was slain, and his body destroyed, and given to the burning flame.

12. As concerning the rest of the beasts, they had their dominion taken away: yet their lives were prolonged for a season and time.

26. But the judgment shall sit, and they shall take away his dominion, to consume and to destroy it unto the end.

27. And the kingdom and dominion, and the greatness of the kingdom under the whole heaven, shall be given to the people of the saints of the Most High, whose kingdom is an everlasting kingdom, and all dominions shall serve and obey him.— *Dan.* 7.

5. And I will come near to you to judgment; and I will be a swift witness against the sorcerers, and against the adulterers, and against false swearers, and against those that oppress the hireling in his wages, the widow, and the fatherless, and that turn aside the stranger from his right, and fear not me, saith the Lord of hosts.—*Mal.* 3.

Judgment to follow the resurrection: 1. For, behold, the day cometh that shall burn as an oven; and all the proud, yea, and all that do wickedly, shall be stubble: and the day that cometh shall burn them up, saith the Lord of hosts, and it shall leave them neither root nor branch.

2. But unto you that fear my name shall the Sun of righteousness arise with healing in his wings; and ye shall go forth, and grow up as calves of the stall.

3. And ye shall tread down the wicked; for they shall be ashes under the soles of your feet in the day that I shall do this, saith the Lord of hosts.—*Mal.* 4.

27. For the Son of man shall come in the glory of his Father with his angels; and then he shall reward every man according to his works. —*Matt.* 16.

28. And Jesus said unto them, Verily I say unto you, that ye which have followed me in the regeneration when the Son of man shall sit in the throne of his glory ye also shall sit upon twelve thrones, judging the twelve tribes of Israel.—*Matt.* 19.

31. When the Son of man shall come in his glory, and all the holy angels with him, then shall he sit upon the throne of his glory:

32. And before him shall be gathered all nations: and he shall separate them one from another, as a shepherd divideth his sheep from the goats:

33. And he shall set the sheep on his right hand, but the goats on the left.

34. Then shall the king say unto them on his right hand, Come ye blessed of my Father, inherit the kingdom prepared for you from the foundation of the world:—*Matt.* 25.

41. Then shall he say also unto them on the *Judgment to* left hand, Depart from me, ye cursed, into *follow the* everlasting fire, prepared for the devil and his *resurrection:* angels:

46. And these shall go away into everlasting punishment: but the righteous into life eternal. —*Matt.* 25.

10. For we must all appear before the judgment seat of Christ; that every one may receive the things done in his body, according to that he hath done, whether it be good or bad.—2 *Cor.* 5.

3. And thinkest thou this, O man, that judgest them which do such things, and doest the same, that thou shalt escape the judgment of God?

6. Who will render to every man according to his deeds:

7. To them who by patient continuance in well doing seek for glory and honor and immortality, eternal life:

8. But unto them that are contentious, and do not obey the truth, but obey unrighteousness, indignation and wrath,

9. Tribulation and anguish, upon every soul of man that doeth evil, of the Jew first, and also of the Gentile:

10. But glory, honor, and peace, to every man that worketh good, to the Jew first, and also to the Gentile:

12. For as many as have sinned without law *Judgment* shall also perish without law: and as many as *according to* have sinned in the law shall be judged by the law; *the law* *of the Gospel:*

13. (For not the hearers of the law are just before God, but the doers of the law shall be justified.)

16. In the day when God shall judge the secrets of men by Jesus Christ according to my gospel.—*Rom.* 2.

Judgment according to the law of the Gospel: 48. He that rejecteth me, and receiveth not my words, hath one that judgeth him: the word that I have spoken, the same shall judge him in the last day.—*John* 12.

Judgment to follow the resurrection: 10. But why dost thou judge thy brother? or why dost thou set at naught thy brother? for we shall all stand before the judgment seat of Christ.—*Rom.* 14.

7. And to you who are troubled rest with us, when the Lord Jesus shall be revealed from heaven with his mighty angels,

8. In flaming fire taking vengeance on them that know not God, and that obey not the gospel of our Lord Jesus Christ:

9. Who shall be punished with everlasting destruction from the presence of the Lord, and from the glory of his power.—2 *Thes.* 1.

26. For if we sin wilfully after that we have received the knowledge of the truth, there remaineth no more sacrifice for sins,

27. But a certain fearful looking for of judgment and fiery indignation, which shall devour the adversaries.

30. For we know him that hath said, Vengeance belongeth unto me, I will recompense, saith the Lord. And again, The Lord shall judge his people.—*Heb.* 10.

14. And Enoch also, the seventh from Adam, prophesied of these, saying, Behold, the Lord cometh with ten thousand of his saints,

15. To execute judgment upon all, and to convince all that are ungodly among them of all their ungodly deeds which they have ungodly committed, and of all their hard speeches which ungodly sinners have spoken against him.—*Jude.*

PRE-EXISTENCE OF SPIRITS.

1. In the beginning was the Word, and the Word was with God, and the Word was God. *Christ's pre-existence*

14. And the Word was made flesh, and dwelt among us, (and we beheld his glory, the glory as of the only begotten of the Father,) full of grace and truth.— *John* 1.

62. What and if ye shall see the Son of man ascend up where he was before?—*John* 6.

28. I came forth from the Father, and am come into the world: again, I leave the world, and go to the Father.—*John* 16.

5. And now, O Father, glorify thou me with thine own self with the glory which I had with thee before the world was.—*John* 17.

20. Who verily was foreordained before the foundation of the world, but was manifest in these last times for you.—1 *Pet.* 1.

13. And no man hath ascended up to heaven, but he that came down from heaven, even the Son of man which is in heaven.—*John* 3.

2. Beloved, now are we the sons of God, and it doth not yet appear what we shall be: but we know that, when he shall appear, we shall be like him; for we shall see him as he is.—1 *John* 3. *Man's divine origin:*

9. Furthermore we have had fathers of our flesh which corrected us, and we gave them reverence: shall we not much rather be in subjection unto the Father of spirits, and live? —*Heb.* 12.

22. And they fell upon their faces, and said, O God, the God of the spirits of all flesh, shall one man sin, and wilt thou be wroth with all the congregation?—*Num.* 16.

Man's divine origin: 16. Let the Lord, the God of the spirits of all flesh, set a man over the congregation.—*Num.* 27.

16. For I will not contend for ever, neither will I be always wroth: for the spirit should fail before me, and the souls which I have made.—*Isa.* 57.

7. Then shall the dust return to the earth as it was: and the spirit shall return unto God who gave it.—*Eccl.* 12.

4. Then the word of the Lord came unto me, saying,

5. Before I formed thee in the belly I knew thee; and before thou camest forth out of the womb I sanctified thee, and I ordained thee a prophet unto the nations.—*Jer.* 1.

Job's pre-existence 4. Where wast thou when I laid the foundations of the earth? declare, if thou hast understanding.

7. When the morning stars sang together, and all the sons of God shouted for joy?—*Job* 38.

Chosen before the foundation of the world: 3. Blessed be the God and Father of our Lord Jesus Christ, who hath blessed us with all spiritual blessings in heavenly places in Christ:

4. According as he hath chosen us in him before the foundation of the world, that we should be holy and without blame before him in love:

5. Having predestinated us unto the adoption of children by Jesus Christ to himself, according to the good pleasure of his will.—*Eph.* 1.

2. In hope of eternal life, which God, that cannot lie, promised before the world began.—*Tit.* 1.

1. And as Jesus passed by, he saw a man which was blind from his birth. *Pre-exist-ence under-stood by the disciples:*

2. And his disciples asked him, saying, Master, who did sin, this man, or his parents, that he was born blind?—*John* 9.

8. But there is a spirit in man: an l the inspiration of the Almighty giveth them under standing.—*Job* 32. *Spirit in man:*

44. It is sown a natural body; it is raised a spiritual body. There is a natural body, and there is a spiritual body.—1 *Cor.* 15. *Spiritual body distinct*

39. Behold my hands and my feet, that it is I myself: handle me, and see; for a spirit hath not flesh and bones, as ye see me have.—*Luke* 24. *Resembling natural body:*

2. I knew a man in Christ above fourteen years ago, (whether in the body, I cannot tell; or whether out of the body, I cannot tell: God knoweth;) such an one caught up to the third heaven. *Possessing intelligence:*

4. How that he was caught up into paradise, and heard unspeakable words, which it is not lawful for a man to utter.—2 *Cor.* 12.

9. And when he had opened the fifth seal, I saw under the altar the souls of them that were slain for the word of God, and for the testimony which they held: *Spirits seen by John:*

10. And they cried with a loud voice, saying, How long, O Lord, holy and true, dost thou not judge and avenge our blood on them that dwell on the earth?

11. And white robes were given unto every one of them; and it was said unto them, that they should rest yet for a little season, until their fellow-servants also and their brethren, that should be killed as they were, should be fulfilled.—*Rev.* 6.

Samuel's spirit called up: 3. Now Samuel was dead, and all Israel had lamented him, and buried him in Ramah, even in his own city. And Saul had put away those that had familiar spirits, and the wizards out of the land.

6. And when Saul enquired of the Lord, the Lord answered him not, neither by dreams, nor by Urim, nor by prophets.

7. Then said Saul unto his servants, Seek me a woman that hath a familiar spirit, that I may go to her, and enquire of her. And his servants said to him, Behold, there is a woman that hath a familiar spirit at En-dor.

11. Then said the woman, Whom shall I bring up unto thee? And he said, Bring me up Samuel.

12. And when the woman saw Samuel, she cried with a loud voice: and the woman spake to Saul, saying, Why hast thou deceived me? for thou art Saul.

13. And the king said unto her, Be not afraid: for what sawest thou? And the woman said unto Saul, I saw gods ascending out of the earth.

14. And he said unto her, What form is he of? And she said an old man cometh up; and he is covered with a mantle. And Saul perceived that it was Samuel, and he stooped with his face to the ground, and bowed himself.

15. And Samuel said to Saul, Why hast thou disquieted me, to bring me up? And Saul answered, I am sore distressed; for the Philistines make war against me, and God is departed from me, and answereth me no more, neither by prophets nor by dreams: therefore I have called thee, that thou mayest make known unto me what I shall do.—1 *Sam.* 28.

7. And there was war in heaven: Michael *Spirits at war:* and his angels fought against the dragon; and the dragon fought and his angels,

8. And prevailed not; neither was their place found any more in heaven.

9. And the great dragon was cast out, that old serpent, called the Devil, and Satan, which deceiveth the whole world: he was cast out into the earth, and his angels were cast out with him.

10. And I heard a loud voice saying in heaven, Now is come salvation, and strength, and the kingdom of our God, and the power of his Christ: for the accuser of our brethren is cast down, which accused them before our God day and night.

11. And they overcame him by the blood of the Lamb, and by the word of their testimony; and they loved not their lives unto the death.

12. Therefore rejoice, ye heavens, and ye that dwell in them. Woe to the inhabitants of the earth and of the sea! for the devil is come down unto you, having great wrath, because he knoweth that he hath but a short time.—*Rev.* 12.

6. And the angels which kept not their first estate, but left their own habitation, he hath reserved in everlasting chains under darkness unto the judgment of the great day.—*Jude.*

53. For this corruptible must put on incor- *Spirit of man immortal:* ruption, and this mortal must put on immortality.

54. So when this corruptible shall have put on incorruption, and this mortal shall have put on immortality, then shall be brought to pass the saying that is written, Death is swallowed up in victory.—1 *Cor.* 15.

PERSONALITY OF GOD.

NOTE.—The idea prevails very generally among professed Christians, that God is an inmaterial Being, existing everywhere in general and nowhere in particular. The first of the "Articles of Religion," as published in the Church of England prayer book, says: "There is but one living and true God, everlasting, without body, parts or passions; of infinite power, wisdom and goodness." Of course, such a being must be a myth, and can exist only in a distorted imagination. This idea of the character of the Deity is not only unreasonable, but unscriptural, for the Bible teaches us that He possesses a body, with the various parts which characterize the body of man, and also such passions as love and hatred:

Christ in the image of the Father:

3. Who being the brightness of his glory, and the express image of his person, and upholding all things by the word of his power, when he had by himself purged our sins, sat down on the right hand of the Majesty on high.—*Heb.* 1.

5. Let this mind be in you, which was also in Christ Jesus:

6. Who, being in the form of God, thought it not robbery to be equal with God:

7. But made himself of no reputation, and took upon him the form of a servant, and was made in the likeness of men:

8. And being found in fashion as a man, he humbled himself, and became obedient unto death, even the death of the cross.—*Phil.* 2.

Man in image of God

26. And God said, Let us make man in our image, after our likeness: and let them have dominion over the fish of the sea, and over the fowl of the air, and over the cattle, and over all the earth, and over every creeping thing that creepeth upon the earth.

27. So God created man in his own image, in the image of God created he him; male and female created he them.—*Gen.* 1.

8. But the tongue can no man tame; it is an unruly evil, full of deadly poison.

Man in image of God

9. Therewith bless we God, even the Father; and therewith curse we men, which are made after the similitude of God.—*Jas.* 3.

1. And the Lord appeared unto him in the plains of Mamre: and he sat in the tent door, in the heat of the day;

The Lord talks and eats with Abraham:

2. And he lifted up his eyes and looked, and lo, three men stood by him: and when he saw them, he ran to meet them from the tent door, and bowed himself toward the ground,

3. And said, My Lord, if now I have found favor in thy sight, pass not away, I pray thee, from thy servant:

4. Let a little water, I pray thee, be fetched, and wash your feet, and rest yourselves under the tree:

5. And I will fetch a morsel of bread, and comfort ye your hearts; after that ye shall pass on: for therefore are ye come to your servant. And they said, So do, as thou hast said.—*Gen.* 18.

24. And Jacob was left alone; and there wrestled a man with him until the breaking of the day.

Wrestles with Jacob:

25. And when he saw that he prevailed not against him, he touched the hollow of his thigh; and the hollow of Jacob's thigh was out of joint, as he wrestled with him.

26. And he said, Let me go for the day breaketh. And he said, I will not let thee go, except thou bless me.

27. And he said unto him, What is thy name? And he said, Jacob.

28. And he said, Thy name shall be called no more Jacob, but Israel: for as a prince hast thou power with God and with men, and hast prevailed.—*Gen.* 32.

9

Seen by Jacob face to face:

29. And Jacob asked him, and said, Tell me, I pray thee, thy name. And he said, Wherefore is it that thou dost ask after my name? And he blessed him there.

30. And Jacob called the name of the place Peniel: for I have seen God face to face, and my life is preserved.—*Gen.* 32.

Seen by Moses and others:

9. Then went up Moses, and Aaron, Nadab, and Abihu, and seventy of the elders of Israel:

10. And they saw the God of Israel: and there was under his feet as it were a paved work of a sapphire stone, and as it were the body of heaven in his clearness.—*Exo.* 24.

Talked with Moses:

7. My servant Moses is not so, who is faithful in all mine house.

8. With him will I speak mouth to mouth, even apparently, and not in dark speeches; and the similtude of the Lord shall he behold: wherefore then were ye not afraid to speak against my servant Moses?—*Num.* 12.

9. And it came to pass, as Moses entered into the tabernacle, the cloudy pillar descended, and stood at the door of the tabernacle, and the Lord talked with Moses.

10. And all the people saw the cloudy pillar stand at the tabernacle door: and all the people rose up and worshipped, every man in his tent door.

11. And the Lord spake unto Moses face to face, as a man speaketh unto his friend.

Parts of the body of the Deity mentioned:

20. And he said, Thou canst not see my face: for there shall no man see me, and live.

21. And the Lord said, Behold, there is a place by me, and thou shalt stand upon a rock:—*Exo.* 33.

22. And it shall come to pass, while my glory passeth by, that I will put thee in a cleft of the rock, and will cover thee with my hand while I pass by:

23. And I will take away mine hand, and thou shalt see my back parts; but my face shall not be seen.—*Exo.* 33.

16. Thine eyes did see my substance, yet being unperfect: and in thy book all my members were written, which in continuance were fashioned, when as yet there was none of them.—*Psal.* 139.

27. Behold, the name of the Lord cometh from far, burning with his anger, and the burden thereof is heavy: his lips are full of indignation, and his tongue as a devouring fire.—*Isa.* 30.

4. The Lord is in his holy temple, the Lord's throne is in heaven: his eyes behold, his eyelids try, the children of men.—*Psal.* 11.

11. As for me, I will behold thy face in righteousness: I shall be satisfied, when I awake, with thy likeness.—*Psal.* 17.

10. And the Lord delivered unto me two tables of stone written with the finger of God; and on them was written according to all the words which the Lord spake with you in the mount out of the midst of the fire in the day of the assembly.—*Deut.* 9.

6. In my distress I called upon the Lord, and cried unto my God: he heard my voice out of his temple, and my cry came before him, even unto his ears.—*Psal.* 18.

.15. The eyes of the Lord are upon the righteous, and his ears are open unto their cry.—*Psal.* 34.

Parts of the body of the Deity mentioned: 16. The face of the Lord is against them that do evil, to cut off the remembrance of them from the earth.—*Psal.* 34.

13. Thou hast a mighty arm: strong is thy hand, and high is thy right hand.—*Psal.* 89.

Seen by Stephen: 55. But he being full of the Holy Ghost, looked up steadfastly into heaven, and saw the glory of God, and Jesus standing on the right hand of God,

56. And said, Behold, I see the heavens opened, and the Son of man standing on the right hand of God.—*Acts* 7.

19. Then answered Jesus and said unto them, Verily, verily, I say unto you, the Son can do nothing of himself, but what he seeth the Father do: for what things soever he doeth, these also doeth the Son likewise.

Passions: 20. For the Father loveth the Son, and sheweth him all things that himself doeth: and he will show him greater works than these, that ye may marvel.—*John* 5.

5. The Lord trieth the righteous: but the wicked and him that loveth violence his soul hateth.

7. For the righteous Lord loveth righteousness; his countenance doth behold the upright.—*Psal.* 11.

37. Behold, I will gather them out of the countries, whither I have driven them in mine anger, and in my fury, and in great wrath; and I will bring them again unto this place, and I will cause them to dwell safely.—*Jer.* 32.

SALVATION FOR THE DEAD.

NOTE.—One of the most common fallacies of the age is a belief that death-bed repentance, or a profession of faith on the Lord Jesus Christ, even at the last moment, and without complying with any of the ordinances of the Gospel, is sufficient to insure salvation. The reply of the Savior to the thief upon the cross is frequently quoted in proof of this, with the idea that the spirit of that penitent sinner went straight to heaven—to the presence of the Father, when it left his body. Connected with this is also a belief that those who have died without having accepted of the Gospel (in whatever age or clime they may have lived, or whether they ever heard the name of the Savior or not), are irredeemably damned.

16. He that believeth and is baptized shall be saved; But he that believeth not shall be damned.—*Mark* 16. *Conditions of salvation:*

5. Jesus answered, Verily, verily, I say unto thee, Except a man be born of water and of the Spirit, he cannot enter into the kingdom of God.—*John* 3.

39. And one of the malefactors which were hanged railed on him, saying, If thou be Christ, save thyself and us. *The thief acknowledges his guilt:*

40. But the other answering rebuked him, saying, Dost not thou fear God, seeing thou art in the same condemnation?

41. And we indeed justly; for we receive the due reward of our deeds: but this man hath done nothing amiss.

42. And he said unto Jesus, Lord, remember me when thou comest into thy kingdom. *His request:*

43. And Jesus said unto him, Verily I say unto thee, To-day shalt thou be with me in Paradise.—*Luke* 23. *The Savior's promise:*

Three days after his crucifixion had not been to heaven:

11. But Mary stood without at the sepulchre weeping: and as she wept, she stooped down, and looked into the sepulchre,

12. And seeth two angels in white sitting, the one at the head, and the other at the feet, where the body of Jesus had lain.

13. And they say unto her, Woman, why weepest thou? She saith unto them, Because they have taken away my Lord, and I know not where they have laid him.

14. And when she had thus said, she turned herself back, and saw Jesus standing, and knew not that it was Jesus.

16. Jesus saith unto her, Mary. She turned herself, and saith unto him, Rabboni; which is to say, Master.

17. Jesus saith unto her, Touch me not; for I am not yet ascended to my Father: but go to my brethren, and say unto them, I ascend unto my Father, and your Father; and to my God, and your God.—*John* 20.

Where he was, and what doing during those three days:

18. For Christ also hath once suffered for sins, the just for the unjust, that he might bring us to God, being put to death in the flesh, but quickened by the Spirit:

19. By which also he went and preached unto the spirits in prison;

20. Which sometime were disobedient, when once the long suffering of God waited in the days of Noah, while the ark was a preparing, wherein few, that is, eight souls were saved by water.—1 *Pet.* 3.

Why he did so:

6. For, for this cause was the gospel preached also to them that are dead, that they might be judged according to men in the flesh, but live according to God in the spirit.—1 *Pet.* 4.

25. Verily, verily, I say unto you, The hour is coming; and now is, when the dead shall hear the voice of the Son of God: and they that hear shall live.—*John* 5. *His visit to the spirits in prison predicted:*

22. And they shall be gathered together, as prisoners are gathered in the pit, and shall be shut up in prison, and after many days shall they be visited.—*Isa.* 24.

6. I the Lord have called thee in righteousness, and will hold thine hand, and will keep thee, and give thee for a covenant of the people, for a light of the Gentiles;

7. To open the blind eyes, to bring out the prisoners from the prison, and them that sit in darkness out of the prison house.—*Isa.* 42.

1. The spirit of the Lord God is upon me; because the Lord hath anointed me to preach good tidings unto the meek; he hath sent me to bind up the brokenhearted, to proclaim liberty to the captives, and the opening of the prison to them that are bound.—*Isa.* 61.

27. He looketh upon men, and if any say, I have sinned, and perverted that which was right, and it profited me not;

28. He will deliver his soul from going into the pit, and his life shall see the light.

30. To bring back his soul from the pit, to be enlightened with the light of the living.--*Job.* 33.

29. Else what shall they do which are baptized for the dead, if the dead rise not at all? why are they then baptized for the dead?—1 *Cor.* 15. *Vicarious work upon the earth for the dead:*

5. Behold, I will send you Elijah the prophet before the coming of the great and dreadful day of the Lord: *Revelation in the last days promised:*

6. And he shall turn the heart of the fathers to the children, and the heart of the children to their fathers, lest I come and smite the earth with a curse.-- *Mal.* 4.

NOTE.—Prof. A. Hinderkoper, a German writer, says: "In the second and third centuries every branch and division of the Christian church, so far as their records enable us to judge, believed that Christ preached to the departed spirits." (Haley's Discrepancies of the Bible.)

Bishop Alfred says: "I understand these words (1 Peter iii, 19) to say that our Lord in his disembodied state, did go to the place of detention of departed spirits, and did there announce his work of redemption; preach salvation in fact, to the disembodied spirits of those who refused to obey the voice of God when the judgment of the flood was hanging over them."

While there are many professors of theology who attempt to explain away the words of Peter, or deny their evident meaning, there are many others who are willing to admit that they mean what they say. The "Apostles' Creed," so frequently recited by the Church of England, states that Christ after being crucified, dead and buried, "descended into hell," and the third day rose again from the dead. The third of the thirty-nine articles of religion accepted by all Episcopalians also says: "As Christ died for us, and was buried, so also is it to be believed, that he went down into hell." Why Christ preached to the dead, though, or how they, not being baptized, could be saved, theologians of the day do not explain; the idea of a vicarious baptism being performed by the living in their behalf is foreign to their creeds. Even the Romish church, as Bishop Milner, in his "End of Religious Controversy," confesses, does not pretend to understand the doctrine of baptism for the dead, which was evidently well understood in Paul's day.

It is not unreasonable to infer that the prayers and penance offered in behalf of the dead by professing Christians during later ages, or other means resorted to for the purpose of redeeming the souls of dead friends from purgatory are perverted relics of the vicarious ordinance incidentally alluded to by Paul, as an argument in favor of the resurrection. The vicarious principle is by no means exceptional in the Gospel. Indeed, it lies at the very foundation of the Christian religion. The Savior did a vicarious work in redeeming mankind from the grave. It was customary also among ancient Israel for the tribe of Levi to engage in ordinances and ceremonies in behalf of the people. The mention of the scapegoat in the sixteenth chapter of Leviticus is another illustration of the same principle. And when the preaching to the spirits in prison is considered in connection with the ordinance of baptism for the dead mentioned by Paul, the vicarious means by which the prison doors are to be opened and salvation extended to those who have died without conforming to the ordinances of the Gospel become apparent. In view of the fact that the ordinance for the benefit of the dead, which existed anciently, had become so entirely lost sight of or changed, and that no person living upon the earth could explain authoritatively what was necessary in this connection, the importance and necessity of revelation upon the subject, such as is promised by Malachi, must be plain to every reasonable mind.

PATRIARCHAL MARRIAGE.

Note.—The traditions and prejudices of centuries, the man-made creeds of the day and the laws of all the nations professing a belief in Christ unitedly inculcate the idea that it is sinful for a man, under any circumstances, to have more than one living and undivorced wife at the same time. A careful perusal of the Scriptures will, however, reveal the fact that this practice which is now considered so heinous is in accordance with the divine law given to the ancient Israelites, that it was engaged in with the sanction and blessing of God by many of the best and most favored men of whom the Bible makes mention, and that never has the principle received the divine condemnation.

7. And if a man sell his daughter to be a maidservant, she shall not go out as the menservants do. *Laws providing for a plurality of wives:*

8. If she please not her master, who hath betrothed her to himself, then shall he let her be redeemed: to sell her unto a strange nation he shall have no power, seeing he hath dealt deceitfully with her.

9. And if he hath betrothed her unto his son, he shall deal with her after the manner of daughters.

10. If he take him another wife; her food, her raiment, and her duty of marriage, shall he not diminish.

11. And if he do not these three unto her, then shall she go out free without money.—*Exo.* 21.

15. If a man hath two wives, one beloved, and another hated, and they have borne him children, both the beloved and the hated; and if the firstborn son be hers that was hated:

16. Then it shall be, when he maketh his sons to inherit that which he hath, that he may not make the son of the beloved firstborn before the son of the hated, which is indeed the firstborn:—*Deut.* 21.

Laws providing for a plurality of wives:

17. But he shall acknowledge the son of the hated for the firstborn, by giving him a double portion of all that he hath: for he is the beginning of his strength; the right of the firstborn is his.— *Deut.* 21.

Plural marriage commanded by divine law:

5. If brethren dwell together, and one of them die, and have no child, the wife of the dead shall not marry without unto a stranger: her husband's brother shall go in unto her, and take her to him to wife, and perform the duty of an husband's brother unto her.— *Deut.* 25.

28. If a man find a damsel that is a virgin, which is not betrothed, and lay hold on her, and lie with her, and they be found;

29. Then the man that lay with her shall give unto the damsel's father fifty shekels of silver, and she shall be his wife; because he hath humbled her, he may not put her away all his days.—*Deut.* 22.

16. And if a man entice a maid that is not betrothed, and lie with her, he shall surely endow her to be his wife.—*Exo.* 22.

Plurality of wives sanctioned by the Lord:

3. And Sarai Abram's wife took Hagar her maid the Egyptian, after Abram had dwelt ten years in the land of Canaan, and gave her to her husband Abram to be his wife.

15. And Hagar bare Abram a son: and Abram called his son's name, which Hagar bare, Ishmael.—*Gen.* 16.

15. And God said unto Abraham, as for Sarai thy wife, thou shalt not call her name Sarai, but Sarah shall her name be.

16. And I will bless her, and give thee a son also of her: yea, I will bless her, and she shall be a mother of nations: kings of people shall be of her.—*Gen.* 17.

17. Then Abraham fell upon his face, and *Plurality of* laughed, and said in his heart, Shall a child be *wives sanc-* born unto him that is an hundred years old? *tioned by the Lord:* and shall Sarah, that is ninety years old, bear?

18. And Abraham said unto God, O that Ishmael might have lived before thee!

19. And God said, Sarah thy wife shall bear thee a son indeed; and thou shalt call his name Isaac: and I will establish my covenant with him for an everlasting covenant, and with his seed after him.

20. And as for Ishmael, I have heard thee: *Polygamous* Behold, I have blessed him, and I will make *son blessed* him fruitful, and will multiply him exceed- *by the Lord:* ingly; twelve princes shall he beget, and I will make him a great nation.—*Gen.* 17.

1. And when Rachel saw that she bare *Jacob and* Jacob no children, Rachel envied her sister; *his four* and said unto Jacob, Give me children or else *wives:* I die.

4. And she gave him Bilhah her handmaid to wife: and Jacob went in unto her.

5. And Bilhah conceived, and bare Jacob a son.

6. And Rachel said, God hath judged me, and hath also heard my voice, and hath given me a son: therefore called she his name Dan.

9. When Leah saw that she had left bearing, she took Zilpah her maid, and gave her Jacob to wife.

17. And God hearkened unto Leah, and she conceived, and bare Jacob the fifth son.

18. And Leah said, God hath given me my hire, because I have given my maiden to my husband: and she called his name Issachar.

22. And God remembered Rachel, and God hearkened to her, and opened her womb.

23. And she conceived, and bare a son; and said, God hath taken away my reproach.—*Gen.* 30.

Saul's wives given to David by the Lord in addition to the wives he already had:

7. And Nathan said to David, Thou art the man. Thus said the Lord God of Israel, I anointed thee king over Israel, and I delivered thee out of the hand of Saul;

8. And I gave thee thy master's house, and thy master's wives into thy bosom, and gave thee the house of Israel and of Judah; and if that had been too little, I would moreover have given unto thee such and such things.—2 *Sam.* 12.

All David's acts approved except in the matter of Uriah:

5. Because David did that which was right in the eyes of the Lord, and turned not aside from anything that he commanded him all the days of his life, save only in the matter of Uriah the Hittite.—1 *Kin.* 15.

Moses marries a Midianitish woman:

21. And Moses was content to dwell with the man: and he gave Moses Zipporah his daughter.—*Exo.* 2.

1. Now Moses kept the flock of Jethro his father-in-law, the priest of Midian: and he led the flock to the backside of the desert, and came to the mountain of God, even to Horeb.—*Exo.* 3.

Marries an Ethiopian wife, and Aaron and Miriam complain of it:

1. And Miriam and Aaron spake against Moses because of the Ethiopian woman whom he had married: for he had married an Ethiopian woman.

2. And they said, Hath the Lord indeed spoken only by Moses? hath he not spoken also by us? And the Lord heard it.

3. (Now the man Moses was very meek, above all the men which were upon the face of the earth.)

4. And the Lord spake suddenly unto Moses, and unto Aaron, and unto Miriam, Come out ye three unto the tabernacle of the congregation. And they three came out.—*Num.* 12.

5. And the Lord came down in the pillar of the cloud, and stood in the door of the tabernacle, and called Aaron and Miriam; and they both came forth.

Reproved and cursed for speaking against Moses:

6. And he said, Hear now my words: If there be a prophet among you, I the Lord will make myself known unto him in a vision, and will speak unto him in a dream.

7. My servant Moses is not so, who is faithful in all mine house.

8. With him will I speak mouth to mouth, even apparently, and not in dark speeches; and the similitude of the Lord shall he behold: wherefo e then were ye not afraid to speak against my servant Moses?

9. And the anger of the Lord was kindled against them; and he departed.

10. And the cloud departed from off the tabernacle; and, behold, Miriam became leprous, white as snow: and Aaron looked upon Miriam, and, behold, she was leprous.—*Num.* 12.

11. Now Heber the Kenite, which was of the children of Hobab the father-in-law of Moses, had severed himself from the Kenites. —*Judg.* 4.

Had a Kenite wife also:

1. Now there was a certain man of Ramath-aim-zophim, of mount Ephraim, and his name was Elkanah:

Polygamous parentage of the prophet Samuel:

2. And he had two wives; the name of the one was Hannah, and the name of the other Peninnah: and Peninnah had children but Hannah had no children.

19. And they rose up in the morning early, and worshipped before the Lord, and returned, and came to their house to Ramah: and Elkanah knew Hannah his wife; and the Lord remembered her.—1 *Sam.* 1.

Polygamous parentage of the prophet Samuel:

20. Wherefore it came to pass, when the time was come about after Hannah had conceived, that she bare a son, and called his name Samuel, saying, Because I have asked him of the Lord.—1 *Sam.* 1.

19. And Samuel grew, and the Lord was with him, and did let none of his words fall to the ground.

20. And all Israel from Dan even to Beersheba knew that Samuel was established to be a prophet of the Lord.

21. And the Lord appeared again in Shiloh: for the Lord revealed himself to Samuel in Shiloh by the word of the Lord.—1 *Sam.* 3.

Polygamy right in the sight of God:

2. And Joash did that which was right in the sight of the Lord all the days of Jehoiada the priest.

3. And Jehoiada took for him two wives; and he begat sons and daughters.

15. But Jehoiada waxed old, and was full of days when he died; an hundred and thirty years old was he when he died.

16. And they buried him in the city of David among the kings, because he had done good in Israel, both toward God, and toward his house.—2 *Chr.* 24.

Gideon's large family not disapproved:

30. And Gideon had threescore and ten sons of his body begotten: for he had many wives.

32. And Gideon the son of Joash died in a good old age, and was buried in the sepulchre of Joash his father, in Ophra of the Abiezrites.

33. And it came to pass, as soon as Gideon was dead, that the children of Israel turned again, and went a whoring after Baalim, and made Baal berith their god.—*Judg.* 8.

2. The beginning of the word of the Lord by Hosea. And the Lord said to Hosea, Go, take unto thee a wife of whoredoms and children of whoredoms: for the land hath committed great whoredom, departing from the Lord.

Hosea told by the Lord to take two wives:

3. So he went and took Gomer the daughter of Diblaim; which conceived, and bare him a son.—*Hos.* 1.

1. Then said the Lord unto me, Go yet, love a woman beloved of her friend, yet an adulteress, according to the love of the Lord towards the· children of Israel, who look to other gods, and love flagons of wine.

3. And I said unto her, Thou shalt abide for me many days; thou shalt not play the harlot, and thou shalt not be for another man: so will I also be for thee.—*Hos.* 3.

1. And in that day seven women shall take hold of one man, saying, We will eat our own bread, and wear our own apparel: only let us be called by thy name, to take away our reproach.

Polygamy predicted

2. In that day shall the branch of the Lord be beautiful and glorious, and the fruit of the earth shall be excellent and comely for them that are escaped of Israel.

3. And it shall come to pass, that he that is left in Zion, and he that remaineth in Jerusalem, shall be called holy, even every one that is written among the living in Jerusalem.—*Isa.* 4.

26. And he said unto them, Verily I say unto you, There is no man that hath left house or parents, or brethren, or wife, or children, for the kingdom of God's sake,

Polygamy implied in the Savior's promise:

30. Who shall not receive manifold more in this present time, and in the world to come life everlasting.—*Luke* 18.

Abraham's works held up as an example: 39. They answered and said unto him, Abraham is our father. Jesus saith unto them, If ye were Abraham's children, ye would do the works of Abraham.

40. But now ye seek to kill me, a man that hath told you the truth, which I have heard of God: this did not Abraham.—*John* 8.

11. And we desire that every one of you do show the same diligence to the full assurance of hope unto the end:

12. That ye be not slothful, but followers of them who through faith and patience inherit the promises.

13. For when God made promises to Abraham, because he could swear by no greater, he sware by himself.

14. Saying, Surely blessing I will bless thee, and multiplying I will multiply thee.—*Heb.* 6.

NOTE.—Many more examples of polygamists might be cited, with the Scriptural mention of whose names or acts there is no word of condemnation. In a number of cases where it is not mentioned that men had more than one wife, we are bound to infer that such was the case from the number of children they are said to have had. For example, Jair is said to have had thirty sons (Judges x, 4); Ibzan had thirty sons and thirty daughters, and Abdon had forty sons (Judges vii, 9, 14). These were judges in Israel, and their acts seem to have gained the divine approval. The number of their children is mentioned as if it were an especial honor to have large families, which agrees with the assertion of the Psalmist (Psalm cxxvii), that "children are an heritage of the Lord," and "blessed is he that hath his quiver full of them." The fact that a sentiment the reverse of this prevails to a great extent in most of the so-called "Christian" nations of the present age, is only an indication that the period of apostasy has arrived which Hosea predicted (iv, 10), when he said, "they shall commit whoredoms and shall not increase, because they have left off to take heed to the Lord."

To find any prohibition of polygamy we must go to human rather than to divine law, and if we trace its history to its inception we will find that it originated in opposition to marriage of any kind. "Christianity" was made a state religion in the year 324, when Constantine, after the death of Licinius, ruled the Roman empire. It has been remarked that "however favorable the protection of the civil magistrate was at that time, as well as in after times, to the Christian religion, yet from hence we must date the misfortunes which have attended the interference of human power, in the establishment of human systems of faith and ceremony; the former of which have been contrary to God's word, the latter utterly subversive of it." Among other things which Constantine did was to abrogate the "ancient Roman laws *Julia* and *Papia* wherein the desire of women and married life were so much privileged and encouraged, and single and unmarried life disadvantaged." (Mede's Works.)

Sozomen, an ancient Greek historian, says (Hist. Eccl. lib, i, chap. ix): "There was an ancient law among the Romans, forbidding those, who after twenty-five years old, were unmarried, to enjoy the like privileges with married ones; and besides many other things, that they should have no benefit by testaments and legacies, unless they were next of kindred: and those who had no children, to have half their goods confiscated. Wherefore the emperor, seeing those who for God's sake were addicted to chastity and virginity to be, for this cause, in a worse condition; he published a law—that both those who lived a single life and those who had no children, should enjoy like privileges with others: yea, he enacted that those who lived in chastity and virginity, should be privileged above them; enabling both sexes, though under years, to make testaments, contrary to the accustomed polity of the Romans."

Mede says of this: "That which the fathers had thus enacted the sons also seconded, and some of the following emperors, by new edicts, till there was no relic left of those ancient privileges wherewith married men had been respected. This was the first step" (he must mean by public authority of the government) "of the disregard of marriage, and the desire of wiving; which was not an absolute prohibition, but a discouragement. No sooner had the Roman bishop and his clergy got the power into their hands, but it grew to an absolute prohibition, not for monks only, but for the whole clergy: which was the highest disrespect that could be to that which God had made honorable among all men."

"Thelyphthora," a most exhaustive work on the subject of plural marriage, published about a century since, the author of which was the learned Dr. Martin Madan, of London, abounds with unanswerable arguments and historical citations which are well worth producing, but limited space forbids the insertion here of any more than the following:

"The first public law in the [Roman] empire against polygamy was at the latter end of the fourth century, about the year 393, by the Emperor Theodosius; this was repealed by the Emperor Valentinian about sixty years afterwards, and the subjects of the empire were permitted to marry as many wives as they pleased." (Vol. 1, p. 211.)

"As for the practice of polygamy amongst the early Christians it was probably very frequent. * * * So it would seem to have been in times long after them, not only among the laity, but the clergy also; for Pope Sylvester, about the year 335, made an ordinance that every Priest should be the husband of one wife

10

only. So in the sixth century, it was enacted in one of the canons of their councils, that if any one is married to many wives, he shall do penance. * * * The learned Selden has proved in his Uxor Hæbraica, that polygamy was allowed, not only amongst the Hebrews, but amongst most other nations throughout the world; doubtless amongst the inhabitants of that vast track of Asia throughout which the Gospel was preached by the great apostle of the Gentiles, where so many Christian churches were planted, as well as in the neighboring states of Greece." (Vol 1, page 192-194.)

"How polygamy became reprobated in the Christian church is easily accounted for, when we consider how early the reprobation of marriage itself began to appear. The Gnostics condemned marriage in the most shocking terms, saying it was of the devil. Better people soon afterwards condemned marriage as unlawful to Christians, and this under a wild notion of greater purity and perfection in keeping from all intercourse with the other sex. This opinion divided itself into many sects, and gave great trouble to the church before it was discountenanced. Still second marriages were held infamous, and called no better than lawful whoredom. Nay, they were not ashamed to write, that, a man's first wife being dead, it was adultery and not marriage to take another. Amidst all this, polygamy must necessarily receive the severest anathema." (P. 291.)

"So far from Jesus Christ ever condemning polygamy, which as a new lawgiver, he is supposed to have done, he never mentioned it during the whole course of his ministry, but left that, as he had all other *moral* actions of men, upon the footing of that law under which he was made, and to which he, for us men, and for our salvation, became subject and obedient unto death." (P. 306.)

"Our chief reformers, Luther, Melancthon, Bucer, Zuinglius, etc., after a solemn consultation at Wittemberg, on the question 'whether for a man to have two wives at once, was contrary to the divine law?' answered unanimously 'that it was not'—and on this authority, Philip the Landgrave of Hesse actually married a second wife, his first being alive." (P. 212.) The language of this council was "The Gospel hath neither recalled nor forbid what was permitted in the law of Moses with respect to marriage."

"We do not worship the same God which the Jews did, or the God we worship doth not disallow nor disapprove polygamy." (P. 280.)

"Josephus says it was the custom of the Jews to live with a plurality of wives—the custom of their country, derived from their fathers." (P. 392.)

"The Jews and Greeks were wont to be married to two or three, and even more wives together." (P. 244.)

"That polygamy was practiced throughout all ages of the Jewish economy, cannot be denied. It is equally evident, that it was the deliberate, open, avowed, and willful practice of the most holy and excellent of the earth, of Abraham, the father of the faithful, the friend of God (Is. xli, 8), as well as of the most illustrious of his children; and this, without the least reproof or rebuke from God; or the most distant hint or expression of his displeasure, either by Moses or any other of the prophets. No trace of sorrow, remorse, or repentance, touching this matter, is to be found in any one instance, and therefore many 'commentators are at a loss to maintain the sinfulness of polygamy, but at the expense of Scripture, reason and common sense." (P. 89.)

"That there were many polygamists among the Gentile converts, as well as among the Jewish, there can be but little doubt; for as Grotius observes: 'Among the Pagans, few nations were content with one wife.'" (Pp. 243-244.)

"If women taken by men already married were not lawful wives in God's sight, then commerce with them was illicit, and the issue must be illegitimate. Whither will this carry us? Even to bastardizing the Messiah himself. Unless an after-taken wife be a lawful wife to the man who takes her, notwithstanding his former wife being living, whether we take our Lord's genealogy on his supposed father's side with St. Matthew, or on his mother's side with St. Luke, Solomon the ancestor of Joseph, and Nathan the ancestor of Mary, through whom our Lord's line runs back to David, being the children of Bathsheba (whom when David married he had also other wives by whom he had children), must fail in their legitimacy." (Vol. 2, p. 14.)

"That polygamy and concubinage were both dispensations of God, both modes of lawful and honorable marriage, is a proposition as clear as the Hebrew scriptures can make it. That polygamy and concubinary contracts are deemed by the Christians null and void, and stamped with the infamy of adultery and whoredom, is as certain as that the canons and decrees of the Church of Rome made them so. The consequences of the former were the preservation of female chastity, and the prevention of female ruin. The consequences of the latter have been and still are the destruction of thousands of both sexes, but more especially the female, in this world and the next." (Vol. 3, pp. 278, 279).

Grotius says: "The Jewish law restrains all filthiness, but allows a plurality of wives to one man." And again; "When God permits a thing in certain cases and to certain persons, or in regard to certain nations, it may be inferred that the thing permitted is not evil in its own nature." * * * "Polygamy, therefore, is not in its own nature, evil and unlawful." He also quotes Persichta Zotertha as saying, "It is very well known that those who pretend a plurality of wives was prohibited, do not understand what the law is."

St. Augustine says: "There was a blameless custom of one man having many wives—for there are many things which at that time might be done in a way of duty, which now cannot be done but licentiously—because, for the sake of multiplying posterity, no law forbade a plurality of wives." Again he says; "It is objected against Jacob that he had four wives," to which he replies; "which, when a custom was not a crime." In another instance he alludes to the custom of having several wives at the same time as an "innocent thing," and observes that "it was prohibited by no law."

Puffendorf says: "The polygamy of the fathers under the old covenant is a reason which ingenuous men must confess to be unanswerable." Again he says: "The Mosaical law was so far from forbidding this custom that it seems in some places to suppose it."

St. Ambrose, speaking of polygamy, says that. "God, in the terrestrial paradise, approved of the marriage of one with one, but without condemning the contrary practice."

St. Chrysostom, speaking of Sarah, says: "She endeavored to comfort her husband, under her barrenness, with children by her handmaid, for such things were not then forbidden." Again he says, "The law permitted a man to have two wives at the same time; in short, great indulgence was granted in those and other particulars."

Bucer, the great reformer, says: "The concubines of the holy fathers were of the lawful kind. And because the Lord will, that the dignities and patrimonies which he has conferred on his people should be preserved, in is altogether to be wished, that this kind of wives, as observed among the holy patriarchs, might be again observed among Christians, and especially in great and illustrious families."

Bellarmine says: "Polygamy is not repugnant to the law of nature, which is divine, that one man might beget and bring up children by more women than one."

Noldius, the eminent Danish theologian of the 17th century, says: "The old Saints who were polygamists did not sin before God, because they had a special and extraordinary dispensation."

Zuinglius says: "The Apostles had made no new law about polygamy, but had left it as they found it."

Theodoret says that "in Abraham's time polygamy was forbidden neither by the law of nature nor by any written law."

"As for the modern Jews," says Leo Mutinensis, "those of them who live in the East still keep up their ancient practice of polygamy."

Bishop Burnet says: "Polygamy was made, in some cases, a duty by Moses' law; when any died without issue, his brother, or nearest kinsman, was to marry his wife, for raising up seed to him; and all were obliged to obey this under the hazard of infamy if they refused; neither is there any exception for such as were married; from whence I may conclude, that what God made necessary in some cases, to any degree, can in no case be sinful in itself, since God is holy in all his ways. And thus far it appears that polygamy is not contrary to the law and nature of marriage."

Lord Bolingbroke, in his published "Works" says: "Polygamy has always prevailed, and still prevails generally, if not universally, as a reasonable indulgence to mankind.   *   *   * Polygamy was allowed by the Mosaical law and was authorized by God himself.   *   *   * The prohibition of polygamy is not only a prohibition of what nature permits in the fullest manner, but of what she requires for the reparation of states exhausted by wars, by plagues, and other calamities. The prohibition is absurd, and the imposition" [of monogamy] "arbitrary. * * * If it" [monogamy] "was the most perfect state there is reason for wonder how the most perfect kind came to be established by an uninspired lawgiver among the nations, whilst the least perfect kind" [polygamy] "had been established by Moses the messenger and prophet of God, among his chosen people."

Milton, in the "First Book on Christian Faith," amply proves, from the Scriptures, the lawfulness of polygamy, and concludes as follows: "Who can believe, either that so many men of the highest character should have sinned through ignorance for so many ages; or that their hearts should have been so hardened; or that God should have tolerated such conduct in his people? Let therefore the rule received among theologians have the same weight here as in other cases: 'The practice of the Saints is the best interpretation of the commandments.' "

"The marriage system of polygamy never formed a part of that ceremonial dispensation which was abrogated by the New Testament; nor has it ever been proved that the New Testament was designed to affect any change in it; but the presumption is that this new dispensation has also left it, as it found it— abiding still in force. If any change were to be made in an institution of such long standing, confirmed by positive law, it could obviously be made only by equally positive and explicit ordinances or enactments of the gospel. But such enactments are wanting. Christ himself was altogether silent in respect to polygamy, not once alluding to it; yet it was practiced at the time of his advent throughout Judea and Galilee, and in all the other countries of Asia and Africa, and without doubt, by some of his own disciples. The Book of the Acts is equally silent as the four Gospels are. No allusion to it is found in any of the sermons or instructions or discussions of the apostles and early saints recorded in that book. It was not because Jesus or the apostles durst not condemn it, had they considered it sinful, that they did not speak of it, for Jesus hesitated not to denounce the sins of hypocrisy, covetousness, and adultery, and even to alter and amend, apparently, the ancient laws respecting divorce and retaliation; but he never rebuked them for their polygamy, nor instituted any change in that system. And this uniform silence, so far as it implies anything, implies approval. John the Baptist was thrown into prison, where he was afterwards beheaded, for reproving King Herod on account of his adultery: and we cannot doubt, that, if he had considered polygamy to be sinful, he would have mentioned it; for Herod's father was, just before that time, living with nine wives, whose names are recorded by Josephus, in his 'Antiquities of the Jews;' but John only reproved him for marrying Herodias, his brother Philip's wife, while his brother was living. He administered the same reproof to Herod that Nathan had formerly done to David, and for similar reasons."— *History and Philosophy of Marriage.*

TITHING.

*Law to an-
ient Israel:* 30. And all the tithe of the land, whether
of the seed of the land, or of the fruit of the
tree, is the Lord's: it is holy unto the Lord.

31. And if a man will at all redeem ought
of his tithes, he shall add thereto the fifth part
thereof.

32. And concerning the tithe of the herd,
or of the flock, even of whatsoever passeth
under the rod, the tenth shall be holy unto the
Lord.

33. He shall not search whether it be good
or bad, neither shall he change it: and if he
change it at all, then both it and the change
thereof shall be holy; it shall not be redeemed.

34. These are the commandments, which the
Lord commanded Moses for the children of
Israel in mount Sinai.—*Lev.* 27.

*To whom
paid:* 21. And, behold, I have given the children
of Levi all the tenth in Israel for an inheritance, for their service which they serve, even
the service of the tabernacle of the congregation.

*Levites also
to give tithes:* 26. Thus speak unto the Levites, and say
unto them, When ye take of the children of
Israel the tithes which I have given you from
them for your inheritance, then ye shall offer
up an heave offering of it for the Lord, even a
tenth part of the tithe.—*Num.* 18.

18. And Melchisedek king of Salem brought
forth bread and wine: and he was the priest of
the most high God.

19. And he blessed him, and said, Blessed
be Abraham of the most high God, possessor of
heaven and earth:—*Gen.* 14.

20. And blessed be the most high God, which hath delivered thine enemies into thy hand. And he gave him tithes of all.—*Gen.* 14.

1. For this Melchisedec, king of Salem, priest of the most high God, who met Abraham returning from the slaughter of the kings, and blessed him; *Abraham pays tithes to Melchisedec:*

2. To whom also Abraham gave a tenth part of all; first being by interpretation King of righteousness, and after that also King of Salem, which is, King of peace.—*Heb.* 7.

5. And verily they that are of the sons of Levi, who received the office of the priesthood, have a commandment to take tithes of the people according to the law, that is, of their brethren, though they come out of the loins of Abraham.—*Heb.* 7. *Levites to receive tithes:*

22. Thou shalt truly tithe all the increase of thy seed, that the field bringeth forth year by year. *All the increase to be tithed:*

23. And thou shalt eat before the Lord thy God, in the place which he shall choose to place his name there, the tithe of thy corn, of thy wine, and of thine oil, and the firstlings of thy herds and of thy flocks; that thou mayest learn to fear the Lord thy God always. *To be eaten in a chosen place:*

24. And if the way be too long for thee, so that thou art not able to carry it; or if the place be too far from thee, which the Lord thy God shall choose to set his name there, when the Lord thy God hath blessed thee:

25. Then shalt thou turn it into money, and bind up the money in thine hand, and shalt go unto the place which the Lord thy God shalt choose:—*Deut.* 14.

The third year's tithes to be laid up. 28. At the end of three years thou shalt bring forth all the tithe of thine increase the same year, and shalt lay it up within thy gates:

Persons to be benefitted by the tithes: 29. And the Levite, (because he hath no part nor inheritance with thee,) and the stranger, and the fatherless, and the widow, which are within thy gates, shall come, and shall eat and be satisfied; that the Lord thy God may bless thee in all the work of thine hand which thou doest.—*Deut.* 14.

Jacob's vow: 22. And this stone, which I have set for a pillar, shall be God's house: and of all that thou shalt give me I will surely give the tenth unto thee.—*Gen.* 28.

Tithe paying revived in Jerusalem, under Nehemiah: 10. And I perceived that the portions of the Levites had not been given them: for the Levites and the singers, that did the work, were fled every one to his field.

11. Then contended I with the rulers, and said, Why is the house of God forsaken? And I gathered them together and set them in their place.

12 Then brought all Judah the tithe of the corn and the new wine and the oil unto the treasuries.—*Neh.* 13.

Israelites, under Hezekiah, pay tithes, and are blessed: 5. And as soon as the commandment came abroad, the children of Israel brought in abundance the firstfruits of corn, wine, and oil, and honey, and of all the increase of the field; and the tithe of all things brought they in abundantly.

6. And concerning the children ef Israel and Judah, that dwelt in the cities of Judah, they also brought in the tithe of oxen and sheep, and the tithe of holy things which were consecrated unto the Lord their God, and laid them by heaps.

9. Then Hezekiah questioned with the priests and the Levites concerning the heaps.—*2 Chr.* 31.

10. And Azariah the chief priest of the house of Zadok answered him, and said, Since the people began to bring the offerings into the house of the Lord, we have had enough to eat, and have left plenty: for the Lord hath blessed his people; and that which is left is this great store.—2 *Chron.* 31.

Israelites, under Heze-kiah, pay tithes, and are blessed:

7. Even from the days of your fathers ye are gone away from mine ordinances, and have not kept them. Return unto me, and I will return unto you, said the Lord of hosts. But ye said, Wherein shall we return?

Accused of robbing God of tithes and offerings:

8. Will a man rob God? Yet ye have robbed me. But ye say, Wherein have we robbed thee? In tithes and offerings.

10. Bring ye all the tithes into the store-house, that there may be meat in mine house, and prove me now herewith, saith the Lord of hosts, if I will not open you the windows of heaven, and pour you out a blessing, that there shall not be room enough to receive it.

Blessing to be gained by obedience:

11. And I will rebuke the devourer for your sakes, and he shall not destroy the fruits of your ground; neither shall your vine cast her fruit before the time in the field, saith the Lord of hosts.—*Mal.* 3.

9. Honor the Lord with thy substance, and with the first-fruits of all thine increase:

10. So shall thy barns be filled with plenty, and thy presses shall burst out with new wine. —*Prov.* 3.

23. Woe unto you, scribes and Pharisees, hypocrites! for ye pay tithe of mint and anise and cummin, and have omitted the weightier matters of the law, judgment, mercy, and faith: these ought ye to have done, and not to leave the other undone.—*Matt.* 23.

Approved by Jesus:

PERSECUTION,

THE HERITAGE OF THE FAITHFUL.

Foretold by the Savior: 22. And ye shall be hated of all men for my name's sake: but he that endureth to the end shall be saved.

23. But when they persecute you in this city, flee ye into another: for verily I say unto you, Ye shall not have gone over the cities of Israel, till the son of man be come.—*Matt.* 10.

9. Then shall they deliver you up to be afflicted, and shall kill you: and ye shall be hated of all nations for my name's sake.—*Matt.* 24.

12. But before all these, they shall lay their hands on you, and persecute you, delivering you up to the synagogues, and into prisons, being brought before kings and rulers for my name's sake.

16. And ye shall be betrayed both by parents, and brethren, and kinsfolks, and friends; and some of you shall they cause to be put to death.—*Luke* 21.

2. They shall put you out of the synagogues: yea, the time cometh, that whosoever killeth you will think that he doeth God service.

3. And these things will they do unto you, because they have not known the Father, nor me.

33. These things I have spoken unto you, that in me ye might have peace. In the world ye shall have tribulation: but be of good cheer; I have overcome the world.—*John* 16.

29. And Jesus answered and said, Verily I say unto you, There is no man that hath left house, or brethren, or sisters, or father, or mother, or wife, or children, or lands, for my sake, and the gospel's,—*Mark* 10.

30. But he shall receive an hundredfold *Foretold by the Savior:* now in this time, houses, and brethren, and sisters, and mothers, and children, and lands, with persecutions; and in the world to come eternal life.—*Mark* 10.

34. Wherefore, behold, I send unto you prophets, and wise men, and scribes; and some of them ye shall kill and crucify, and some of them shall ye scourge in your synagogues, and persecute them from city to city:

35. That upon you may come all the righteous blood shed upon the earth, from the blood of righteous Abel unto the blood of Zacharias, son of Barachias, whom ye slew between the temple and the altar.—*Matt.* 23.

12. Beloved, think it not strange concern- *Promised* ing the fiery trial which is to try you, as though *by Peter:* some strange thing happened unto you:

13. But rejoice, inasmuch as ye are partakers of Christ's sufferings; that, when his glory shall be revealed, ye may be glad also with exceeding joy.—1 *Pet.* 4.

12. Yea, and all that will live godly in Christ *By Paul:* Jesus shall suffer persecution.—2 *Tim.* 3.

10. Blessed are they which are persecuted *Consolation* for righteousness' sake: for theirs is the king- *in persecution:* dom of heaven.

11. Blessed are ye, when men shall revile you, and persecute you, and shall say all manner of evil against you falsely, for my sake.

12. Rejoice, and be exceeding glad: for great is your reward in heaven: for so persecuted they the prophets which were before you.— *Matt.* 5.

14. But and if ye suffer for righteousness' sake, happy are ye: and be not afraid of their terror, neither be troubled.—1 *Pet.* 3.

Consolation in persecution: 22. Blessed are ye, when men shall hate you, and when they shall separate you from their company, and shall reproach you, and cast out your name as evil, for the Son of man's sake.

23. Rejoice ye in that day, and leap for joy: for, behold, your reward is great in heaven: for in the like manner did their fathers unto the prophets.

26. Woe unto you, when all men shall speak well of you! for so did their fathers to the false prophets.—*Luke* 6.

14. If ye be reproached for the name of Christ, happy are ye; for the spirit of glory and of God resteth upon you: on their part he is evil spoken of, but on your part he is glorified.

19. Wherefore let them that suffer according to the will of God commit the keeping of their souls to him in well doing, as unto a faithful Creator.—1 *Pet.* 4.

13. And one of the elders answered, saying unto me, What are these which are arrayed in white robes? and whence came they?

14. And I said unto him, sir, thou knowest. And he said to me, These are they which came out of great tribulation, and have washed their robes, and made them white in the blood of the Lamb.—*Rev.* 7.

Endured by the disciples of Christ: 9. For I think that God hathset forth us the apostles last, as it were appointed to death: for we are made a spectacle to the world, and to angels, and unto men.

10. We are fools for Christ's sake, but ye are wise in Christ; we are weak, but ye are strong; ye are honorable, but we are despised. —1 *Cor.* 4.

11. Even unto this present hour we both *Endured by* hunger, and thirst, and are naked, and are *the disciples* buffeted, and have no certain dwelling place; *of Christ:*

12. And labor, working with our own hands: being reviled, we bless; being persecuted, we suffer it:

13. Being defamed, we intreat: we are made as the filth of the world, and are the offscouring of all things unto this day.—1 *Cor.* 4.

8. We are troubled on every side, yet not distressed; we are perplexed, but not in despair;

9. Persecuted, but not forsaken; cast down, but not destroyed.

17. For our light affliction, which is but for a moment, worketh for us a far more exceeding and eternal weight of glory.—2 *Cor.* 4.

24. Of the Jews five times received I forty stripes save one.

25. Thrice was I beaten with rods, once was I stoned, thrice I suffered shipwreck, a night and a day I have been in the deep.—2 *Cor.* 11.

11. Persecutions, afflictions, which came unto me at Antioch, at Iconium, at Lystra; what persecutions I endured: but out of them all the Lord delivered me.—2 *Tim.* 3.

36. And others had trial of cruel mockings *By the* and scourgings, yea, moreover of bonds and *ancient* imprisonment: *Prophets:*

37. They were stoned, they were sawn asunder, were tempted, were slain with the sword: they wandered about in sheepskins and goatskins; being destitute, afflicted, tormented;

38. (Of whom the world was not worthy:) they wandered in deserts, and in mountains, and in dens and caves of the earth.—*Heb.* 11.

The prophets an example: 10. Take, my brethren, the prophets, who have spoken in the name of the Lord, for an example of suffering affliction, and of patience. —*Jas.* 5.

19. For this is thankworthy, if a man for conscience toward God endure grief, suffering wrongfully.

20. For what glory is it, if, when ye be buffeted for your faults, ye shall take it patiently? but if, when ye do well, and suffer for it, ye take it patiently, this is acceptable with God.

Christ an example: 21. For even hereunto were ye called: because Christ also suffered for us, leaving us an example, that ye should follow his steps:

22. Who did no sin, neither was guile found in his mouth:

23. Who, when he was reviled, reviled not again; when he suffered, he threatened not; but committed himself to him that judgeth righteously.—1 *Pet.* 2.

Why the righteous are persecuted: 18. If the world hate you, ye know that it hated me before it hated you.

19. If ye were of the world, the world would love his own: but because ye are not of the world, but I have chosen you out of the world, therefore the world hateth you.

20. Remember the word that I said unto you, The servant is not greater than his lord. If they have persecuted me, they will also persecute you; if they have kept my saying, they will keep yours also.

21. But all these things will they do unto you for my name's sake, because they know not him that sent me.—*John* 15.

14. I have given them thy word; and the world hath hated them, because they are not of the world, even as I am not of the world. —*John* 17.

DOOM OF APOSTATES.

28. Verily I say unto you, All sins shall be forgiven unto the sons of men, and blasphemies wherewith soever they shall blaspheme: *Sin against the Holy Ghost not to be forgiven:*

29. But he that shall blaspheme against the Holy Ghost hath never forgiveness, but is in danger of eternal damnation.—*Mark* 3.

47. And that servant which knew his lord's will, and prepared not himself, neither did according to his will, shall be beaten with many stripes.—*Luke* 12. *Responsibility with knowledge:*

4. For it is impossible for those who were once enlightened, and have tasted of the heavenly gift, and were made partakers of the Holy Ghost. *Hopeless condition of apostates:*

5. And have tasted the good word of God, and the powers of the world to come,

6. If they shall fall away, to renew them again unto repentance; seeing they crucify to themselves the Son of God afresh, and put him to an open shame.—*Heb.* 6.

26. For if we sin wilfully after that we have received the knowledge of the truth, there remaineth no more sacrifice for sins.

27. But a certain fearful looking for of judgment and fiery indignation, which shall devour the adversaries.—*Heb.* 10.

20. For if after they have escaped the pollutions of the world through the knowledge of the Lord and Savior Jesus Christ, they are again entangled therein, and overcome, the latter end is worse with them than the beginning.

21. For it had been better for them not to have known the way of righteousness, than, after they have known it, to turn from the holy commandment delivered unto them.— 2 *Pet.* 2.

LATTER-DAY REVELATION AND MIRACLES.

NOTE.—Why should the Lord not reveal His will to man now as in former ages? Why should He not visit men upon the earth and talk with them as he did with Abraham, Moses and others? Why does He not call men directly by His voice as He did Moses, Samuel and Paul? Why should He not send angels to deliver heavenly messages to men now as He did to Gideon, Zacharias and Cornelius? Why does he not enlighten men by means of heavenly visions, as He did Jacob, Peter, Paul and John? Why does He not now inspire prophets to predict with certainty coming events, to declare His will and to interpret dreams and visions and unknown languages, as did Daniel? Why are not miracles and signs made manifest through the power of God now, as in the days of Christ and His Apostles? Surely it is no more unreasonable to expect these things now than in any former age, for, according to the Bible, they are to occur in the last days.

Why revelation ceased: 1. Behold, the Lord's hand is not shortened, that it cannot save; neither his ear heavy, that it cannot hear:

2. But your iniquities have separated between you and your God, and your sins have hid his face from you, and he will not hear.—*Isa.* 59.

Famine for the word of God predicted: 11. Behold, the days come, saith the Lord God, that I will send a famine in the land, not a famine of bread, nor a thirst for water, but of hearing the words of the Lord.

12. And they shall wander from sea to sea, and from the north even to the east, they shall run to and fro to seek the word of the Lord, and shall not find it.—*Amos* 8.

Necessity of revelation: 22. All things are delivered unto me of my Father: and no man knoweth who the Son is, but the Father; and who the Father is, but the Son, and he to whom the Son will reveal him.—*Luke* 10.

4. But thou, O Daniel, shut up the words, *When to be* and seal the book, even to the time of the end: *expected:* many shall run to and fro, and knowledge shall be increased.—*Dan.* 12.

2. And the Lord answered me, and said, Write the vision, and make it plain upon tables, that he may run that readeth it.

3. For the vision is yet for an appointed time, but at the end it shall speak, and not lie: though it tarry, wait for it; because it will surely come, it will not tarry.—*Hab.* 2.

10. Many shall be purified, and made white, *Who are to* and tried: but the wicked shall do wicke ly: *receive it:* and none of the wicked shall understand; but the wise shall understand.—*Dan.* 12.

14. The secret of the Lord is with them that fear him; and he will show them his covenant.—*Ps.* 25.

7. Surely the Lord God will do nothing, but he revealeth his secret unto his servants the prophets.

8. The lion hath roared, who will not fear? the Lord God hath spoken, who can but prophesy?—*Amos* 3.

3. And I will give power unto my two wit- *Prophets* nesses, and they shall prophesy a thousand two *to come:* hundred and threescore days, clothed in sackcloth.—*Rev.* 11.

6. And I saw another angel fly in the midst *An angel to* of heaven, having the everlasting gospel to *bring the* preach unto them that dwell on the earth, and *Gospel:* to every nation, and kindred, and tongue, and people.—*Rev.* 14.

11

*Revelation
promised:* 4. And I heard another voice from heaven, saying, Come out of her, my people, that ye be not partakers of her sins, and that ye receive not of her plagues.

5. For her sins have reached unto heaven, and God hath remembered her iniquities.—*Rev.* 18.

6. Therefore my people shall know my name: therefore they shall know in that day that I am he that doth speak: behold, it is I.—*Isa.*52.

14. Turn, O backsliding children, saith the Lord; for I am married unto you: and I will take you one of a city and two of a family, and I will bring you to Zion:

15. And I will give you pastors according to mine heart, which shall feed you with knowledge and understanding.—*Jer.* 3.

28. And it shall come to pass afterward, that I will pour out my spirit upon all flesh; and your sons and your daughters shall prophesy, your old men shall dream dreams, your young men shall see visions:

29. And also upon the servants and upon the handmaids in those days will I pour out my spirit.—*Joel* 2.

*A new
covenant:* 4. Hearken unto me, my people; and give ear unto me, O my nation: for a law shall proceed from me, and I will make my judgment to rest for a light of the people.—*Isa.*51.

31. Behold, the days come, saith the Lord, that I will make a new covenant with the house of Israel, and with the house of Judah:

32. Not according to the covenant that I made with their fathers in the day that I took them by the hand to bring them out of the land of Egypt; which my covenant they brake, although I was an husband unto them, saith the Lord:—*Jer.* 31.

33. But this shall be the covenant that I *A new* will make with the house of Israel; After *covenant:* those days, saith the Lord, I will put my law in their inward parts, and write it in their hearts; and will be their God, and they shall be my people.—*Jer.* 31.

26. Moreover I will make a covenant of peace with them; it shall be an everlasting covenant with them: and I will place them, and multiply them, and will set my sanctuary in the midst of them for evermore.

28. And the heathen shall know that I the Lord do sanctify Israel, when my sanctuary shall be in the midst of them for evermore.— *Ezek.* 37.

35. And I will bring you into the wilderness of the people, and there will I plead with you face to face.

36. Like as I pleaded with your fathers in the wilderness of the land of Egypt, so will I plead with you, saith the Lord God.

37. And I will cause you to pass under the rod, and I will bring you into the bond of the covenant.—*Ezek.* 20.

20. And the Redeemer shall come to Zion, *Redeemer to* and unto them that turn from transgression in *come to Zion:* Jacob, saith the Lord.

21. As for me, this is my covenant with them, saith the Lord; My spirit that is upon thee, and my words which I have put in thy mouth, shall not depart out of thy mouth, nor out of the mouth of thy seed, nor out of the mouth of thy seed's seed, saith the Lord, from henceforth and forever.—*Isa.* 59.

The Church to be built on the rock of revelation:

17. And Jesus answered and said unto him, Blessed art thou Simon Bar-jona: for flesh and blood hath not revealed it unto thee, but my Father which is in heaven.

18. And I say unto thee, that thou art Peter, and upon this rock I will build my church; and the gates of hell shall not prevail against it.—*Matt.* 16.

Kingdom foretold by Daniel:

44. And in the days of these kings shall the God of heaven set up a kingdom, which shall never be destroyed: and the kingdom shall not be left to other people, but it shall break in pieces and consume all these kingdoms, and it shall stand for ever.—*Dan.* 2.

Revelation promised:

5. Behold, I will bring it health and cure, and I will cure them, and will reveal unto them the abundance of peace and truth.—*Jer.* 33.

8. I will hear what God the Lord will speak: for he will speak peace unto his people, and to his saints: but let them not turn again to folly.

Truth to spring out of the earth:

11. Truth shall spring out of the earth; and righteousness shall look down from heaven.—*Psal.* 85.

8. Drop down, ye heavens, from above, and let the skies pour down righteousness: let the earth open, and let them bring forth salvation, and let righteousness spring up together; I the Lord have created it.—*Isa.* 45.

4. And thou shalt be brought down, and shalt speak out of the ground, and thy speech shall be low out of the dust, and thy voice shall be, as of one that hath a familiar spirit, out of the ground, and thy speech shall whisper out of the dust.—*Isa.* 29.

16. Moreover, thou son of man, take thee *The sticks of* one stick, and write upon it, For Judah, and *Judah and* for the children of Israel his companions: then *Ephraim:* take another stick, and write upon it, For Joseph, the stick of Ephraim, and for all the house of Israel his companions:

17. And join them one to another into one stick; and they shall become one in thine hand.

18. And when the children of thy people shall speak unto thee, saying, Wilt thou not show us what thou meanest by these?

19. Say unto them, Thus saith the Lord God; Behold, I will take the stick of Joseph, which is in the hand of Ephraim, and the tribes of Israel his fellows, and will put them with him, even with the stick of Judah, and make them one stick, and they shall be one in mine hand.—*Ezek.* 37.

NOTE.—When it is understood that the ancients were in the habit of writing upon parchment or papyrus, and rolling the same upon a stick, for convenience, it will be readily perceived that "stick." as here mentioned, means a record, or book. It was sometimes also called a "roll." The Lord, upon one occasion, commanded the prophet Jeremiah to take "a roll of a book" and write therein the words that he had spoken (See Jer. xxxvi, 1, 2, 11).

11. Because Ephraim hath made many altars *Law written* to sin, altars shall be unto him to sin. *to Ephraim:*

12. I have written to him the great things of my law, but they were counted as a strange thing.—*Hos.* 8.

11. And the vision of all is become unto *A book that* you as the words of a book that is sealed, *is sealed:* which men deliver to one that is learned, saying, Read this, I pray thee: and he saith, I cannot; for it is sealed:

12. And the book is delivered to him that is not learned, saying, Read this, I pray thee: and he saith, I am not learned.—*Isa.* 29.

A marvelous work to be done: 13. Wherefore the Lord saith, Forasmuch as this people draw near me with their mouth, and with their lips do honor me, but have removed their heart far from me, and their fear toward me is taught by the precept of men.

14. Therefore, behold, I will proceed to do a marvelous work among this people, even a marvelous work and a wonder: for the wisdom of their wise men shall perish, and the understanding of their prudent men shall be hid.

18. And in that day shall the deaf hear the words of the book, and the eyes of the blind shall see out of obscurity, and out of darkness.

13. The meek also shall increase their joy in the Lord, and the poor among men shall rejoice in the Holy One of Israel.

22. Therefore thus saith the Lord, who redeemed Abraham, concerning the house of Jacob, Jacob shall not now be ashamed, neither shall his face now wax pale.

23. But when he seeth his children, the work of mine hands, in the midst of him, they shall sanctify my name, and sanctify the Holy One of Jacob, and shall fear the God of Israel.

24. They also that erred in spirit shall come to understanding, and they that murmured shall learn doctrine.—*Isa.* 29.

Seed of Israel to be known: 8. For I the Lord love judgment, I hate robbery for burnt offering; and I will direct their work in truth, and I will make an everlasting covenant with them.

8. And their seed shall be known among the Gentiles, and their offspring among the people: all that see them shall acknowledge them, that they are the seed which the Lord hath blessed. —*Isa.* 61.

16. And other sheep I have, which are not *Other sheep:* of this fold: them also I must bring, and they shall hear my voice; and there shall be one fold, and one shepherd.— *John* 10.

5. Behold, I will send you Elijah the prophet *Elijah to be* before the coming of the great and dreadful *revealed:* day of the Lord:

6. And he shall turn the heart of the fatheis to the children, and the heart of the children to the fathers, lest I come and smite the earth with a curse.—*Mal.* 4.

17. And these signs shall follow them that *Unlimited* believe; In my name shall they cast out devils; *promise of signs to* they shall speak with new tongues; *believers*

18. They shall take up serpents; and if they drink any deadly thing, it shall not hurt them; they shall lay hands on the sick, and they shall recover.—*Mark* 16.

38. Then Peter said unto them, Repent, and *A com-* be baptized every one of you in the name of *prehensive promise:* Jesus Christ for the remission of sins, and ye shall receive the gift of the Holy Ghost.

39. For the promise is unto you, and to your children, and to all that are afar off, even as many as the Lord our God shall call.—*Acts* 2.

7. But the manifestation of the Spirit is *How the* given to every man to profit withal. *Spirit was*

8. For to one is given by the Spirit the *manifested in the days of* word of wisdom; to another the word of knowl- *the apostles:* edge by the same Spirit;

9. To another faith by the same Spirit; to another the gift of healing by the same Spirit:

10. To another the working of miracles; to another prophecy; to another discerning of spirits; to another diverse kinds of tongues; to another the interpretation of tongues:

11. But all these worketh that one and the selfsame Spirit, dividing to every man severally as he will.—1 *Cor.* 12.

To continue until that which is per- fect is come: 8. Charity never faileth: but whether there be prophecies, they shall fail; whether there be tongues, they shall cease; whether there be knowledge, it shall vanish away.

9. For we know in part, and we prophecy in part.

10. But when that which is perfect is come, then that which is in part shall be done away.

12. For now we see through a glass darkly; but then face to face: now I know in part; but then shall I know even as also I am known.— 1 *Cor.* 13.

Marvelous work to be done in latter days: 14. Therefore, behold, the days come, saith the Lord, that it shall no more be said, The Lord liveth, that brought up the children of Israel out of the land of Egypt;

15. But, the Lord liveth, that brought up the children of Israel from the land of the north, and from all the lands whither he had driven them: and I will bring them again into their land that I gave unto their fathers.— *Jer.* 16.

Miracles: 15. And the Lord shall utterly destroy the tongue of the Egyptian sea; and with his mighty wind shall he shake his hand over the river, and shall smite it in the seven streams, and make men go over dry shod.

16. And there shall be an highway for the remnant of his people, which shall be left, from Assyria; like as it was to Israel in the day that he came up out of the land of Egypt.—*Isa.*11.

18. Remember ye not the former things, neither consider the things of old.

19. Behold, I will do a new thing; now it shall spring forth; shall ye not know it? I will even make a way in the wilderness, and rivers in the desert.—*Isa.* 43.

4. Say to them that are of a fearful heart, *Miracles:*
Be strong, fear not: behold, your God will
come with vengeance, even God with a recompense; he will come and save you.

5. Then the eyes of the blind shall be opened,
and the ears of the deaf shall be unstopped.

6. Then shall the lame man leap as an hart,
and the tongue of the dumb sing: for in the
wilderness shall waters break out, and streams
in the desert.

7. And the parched ground shall become a
pool, and the thirsty lands springs of water: in
the habitation of dragons, where each lay, shall
be grass with reeds and rushes.—*Isa.* 35.

4. Every valley shall be exalted, and every
mountain and hill shall be made low: and the
crooked shall be made straight, and the rough
places plain:

5. And the glory of the Lord shall be revealed, and all flesh shall see it together: for
the mouth of the Lord hath spoken it.—
Isa. 40.

17. When the poor and needy seek water, *Miracles ye*
and there is none, and their tongue faileth for *to come:*
thirst, I the Lord will hear them, I the God of
Israel will not forsake them.

18. I will open rivers in high places, and
fountains in the midst of the valleys: I will
make the wilderness a pool of water, and the
dry land springs of water.

19. I will plant in the wilderness the cedar,
the shittah tree, and the myrtle, and the oil
tree; I will set in the desert the fir tree, and
the pine, and the box tree together:

20. That they may see, and know, and consider, and understand together, that the hand
of the Lord hath done this, and the Holy One
of Israel hath created it.—*Isa.* 41.

Miracles yet to come: 3. Then shall the Lord go forth, and fight against those nations, as when he fought in the day of battle.

4. And his feet shall stand in that day upon the mount of Olives, which is before Jerusalem on the east, and the mount of Olives shall cleave in the midst thereof toward the east and toward the west, and there shall be a very great valley; and half of the mountain shall remove toward the north, and half of it toward the south.

5. And ye shall flee to the valley of the mountains; for the valley of the mountains shall reach unto Azal: yea, ye shall flee, like as ye fled from before the earthquake in the days of Uzziah king of Judah: and the Lord my God shall come, and all the Saints with thee.

6. And it shall come to pass in that day, that the light shall not be clear, nor dark.—*Zech.* 14.

30. And I will show wonders in the heavens and in the earth, blood, and fire, and pillars of smoke.

31. The sun shall be turned into darkness, and the moon into blood, before the great and terrible day of the Lord come.—*Joel* 2.

29. Immediately after the tribulation of those days, shall the sun be darkened, and the moon shall not give her light, and the stars shall fall from heaven, and the powers of the heavens shall be shaken:

30. And then shall appear the sign of the Son of man in heaven: and then shall all the tribes of the earth mourn, and they shall see the Son of man coming in the clouds of heaven with power and great glory.—*Matt.* 24.

THE PASSOVER OR SACRAMENT.

4. In the fourteenth day of the first month *When to be kept:* at even is the Lord's passover.—*Lev.* 23.

14. And this day shall be unto you for a *A feast by an* memorial; and ye shall keep it a feast to the *ordinance.* Lord throughout your generations: ye shall keep it a feast by an ordinance forever.—*Exo.* 12.

7. Purge out therefore the old leaven, that *Type of* ye may be a new lump, as ye are unleavened. *Christ's death:* For even Christ our passover is sacrificed for us:—1 *Cor.* 5.

7. Then came the day of unleavened bread, *Observed by* when the passover must be killed. *Christ and His Apostles:*

8. And he sent Peter and John, saying, Go and prepare us for the passover, that we may eat.

14. And when the hour was come, he sat down, and the twelve apostles with him.

15. And he said unto them. With desire I have desired to eat this passover with you before I suffer.

16. For I say unto you, I will not any more eat thereof, until it be fulfilled in the kingdom of God.

17. And he took the cup, and gave thanks, and said, Take this, and divide it among yourselves.

18. For I say unto you, I will not drink of the fruit of the vine, until the kingdom of God shall come.

19. And he took bread, and gave thanks, and brake it, and gave unto them, saying, This is my body which is given for you: this do in remembrance of me.—*Luke* 22.

*Observed by
Christ and
His Apostles:* 20. Likewise also the cup after supper, saying, This cup is the new testament in my blood, which is shed for you.— *Luke* 22.

*A Holy
Sacrament:* 24. And when he had given thanks, he brake it, and said, Take, eat: this is my body, which is broken for you: this do in remembrance of me.

25. After the same manner also he took the cup, when he had supped, saying, This cup is the new testament in my blood: this do ye, as oft as ye drink it, in remembrance of me.

26. For as often as ye eat this bread, and drink this cup, ye do shew the Lord's death till he come.

27. Wherefore whosoever shall eat this bread, and drink this cup of the Lord, unworthily, shall be guilty of the body and blood of the Lord.

28. But let a man examine himself, and so let him eat of that bread, and drink of that cup.

29. For he that eateth and drinketh unworthily, eateth and drinketh damnation to himself, not discerning the Lord's body.

30. For this cause many are weak and sickly among you, and many sleep.

33. Wherefore, my brethren, when ye come together to eat, tarry one for another.

34. And if any man hunger, let him eat at home: that ye come not together unto condemnation. And the rest will I set in order when I come.—1 *Cor.* 11.

*Kept by the
disciples:* 46. And they, continuing daily with one accord in the temple, and breaking bread from house to house, did eat their meat with gladness and singleness of heart.—*Acts* 2.

LOST SCRIPTURE.

SCRIPTURE MENTIONED BUT NOT FOUND IN THE BIBLE.

NOTE.—Many people repudiate modern revelation, claiming that the canon of scripture is full and that the Bible contains the whole word of God. The fallacy of such an idea must be apparent when the number of sacred writings mentioned but not found in the Bible are considered, which perhaps if found would be quite as valuable as any the Bible contains.

4. And Moses wrote all the words of the *Book of the* Lord, and rose up early in the morning, and *Covenant:* builded an altar under the hill, and twelve pillars, according to the twelve tribes of Israel.

7. And he took the book of the covenant, and read in the audience of the people: and they said, All that the Lord hath said will we do, and be obedient.—*Exo.* 24.

14. Wherefore it is said in the book of the *Of the Wars:* wars of the Lord, What he did in the Red sea, and in the brooks of Arnon.—*Num.* 21.

13. And the sun stood still, and the moon *Of Jasher:* stayed, until the people had avenged themselves upon their enemies. Is not this written in the book of Jasher? So the sun stood still in the midst of heaven, and hasted not to go down about a whole day.—*Josh.* 10.

25. Then Samuel told the people the man- *Written by* ner of the kingdom, and wrote it in a book, *Samuel:* and laid it up before the Lord. And Samuel sent all the people away, every man to his house.—1 *Sam.* 10.

32. And he spake three thousand proverbs: *By Solomon:* and his songs were a thousand and five.

33. And he spake of trees, from the cedar tree that is in Lebanon even unto the hyssop that springeth out of the wall: he spake also of beasts and of fowl, and of creeping things, and of fishes.—1 *Kin.* 4.

By Solomon: 34. And there came of all people to hear the wisdom of Solomon, from all kings of the earth, which had heard of his wisdom.—1 *Kin.* 4.

Books of the Acts of Solomon: 41. And the rest of the acts of Solomon, and all that he did, and his wisdom, are they not written in the book of the acts of Solomon?—1 *Kin.* 11.

Books of Nathan and Gad: 29. Now the acts of David the king, first and last, behold, they are written in the book of Samuel the seer, and in the book of Nathan the prophet, and in the book of Gad the seer.

30. With all his reign and his might, and the times that went over him, and over Israel, and over all the kingdoms of the countries.— 1 *Chr.* 29.

Prophecy of Ahijah, and Visions of Iddo: 29. Now the rest of the acts of Solomon, first and last, are they not written in the book of Nathan the prophet, and in the prophecy of Ahijah the Shilonite, and in the visions of Iddo the seer against Jeroboam the son of Nebat.—2 *Chr.* 9.

Book of Shemaiah: 15. Now the acts of Rehoboam, first and last, are they not written in the book of Shemaiah the prophet, and of Iddo the seer concerning genealogies? And there were wars between Rehoboam and Jeroboam continually. —2 *Chr.* 12.

Story of Iddo: 22. And the rest of the acts of Abijah, and his ways, and his sayings, are written in the story of the prophet Iddo.—2 *Chr.* 13.

Book of Jehu: 34. Now the rest of the acts of Jehoshaphat first and last, behold, they are written in the book of Jehu the son of Hanani, who is mentioned in the book of the kings of Israel.—2 *Chr.* 20.

22. Now the rest of the acts of Uzziah, first *Acts of* and last, did Isaiah the prophet, the son of *Uzziah:* Amoz, write.—2 *Chr.* 26.

19. His prayer also, and how God was in- *Sayings of* treated of him, and all his sins, and his trespass, *the Seers:* and the places wherein he built high places, and set up groves and graven images, before he was humbled: behold, they are written among the sayings of the seers.—2 *Chr.* 33.

1. Forasmuch as many have taken in hand *A declara-* to set forth in order a declaration of those *tion by many* things which are most surely believed among us.—*Luke* 1.

9. I wrote unto you in an epistle not to *Missing* company with fornicators.—*Cor.* 5. *Epistle:*

8. And the scripture, forseeing that God *Scripture* would justify the heathen through faith, *which* preached before the gospel unto Abraham, *preached* saying, In thee shall all nations be blessed.— *to Abraham:* *Gal.* 3.

1. For this cause I Paul, the prisoner of Jesus Christ for you Gentiles,

2. If ye have heard of the dispensation of the grace of God which is given me to youward:

3. How that by revelation he made known *Former* unto me the mystery, as I wrote afore in few *epistle to the* words. *Ephesians:*

4. Whereby, when ye read, ye may understand my knowledge in the mystery of Christ,

5. Which in other ages was not made known unto the sons of men, as it is now revealed unto his holy apostles and prophets by the Spirit.—*Eph.* 3.

16. And when this epistle is read among *Epistle from* you, cause that it be read also in the church of *Laodicea:* the Laodiceans; and that ye likewise read the epistle from Laodicea.—*Col.* 4.

Former epistle by Jude:

3. Beloved, when I gave all diligence to write unto you of the common salvation, it was needful for me to write unto you, and exhort you that you should earnestly contend for the faith which was once delivered unto the saints.

Enoch's prophecies:

14. And Enoch also, the seventh from Adam, prophesied of these, saying, Behold, the Lord cometh with ten thousand of his saints,

15. To execute judgment upon all, and to convince all that are ungodly among them of all their ungodly deeds which they have ungodly committed, and of all their hard speeches which ungodly sinners have spoken against him. —*Jude.*